Also by John Adam Wasowicz

Daingerfield Island
Jones Point

SLATERS LANE

John Adam Wasowicz

SLATERS LANE

Copyright © John Adam Wasowicz, 2020 All Rights Reserved. No part of this book may be reproduced in any manner without written permission from the publisher and author except in the case of brief quotations embodied in critical articles or reviews. Address inquiries to the publisher or author.

Publisher: Clarinda Harriss
Editor: Charles Rammelkamp
Graphic design: Ace Kieffer
Cover art: Alex Herron Wasowicz

Slaters Lane is a work of fiction. Names, characters, places, and incidents are the products of the author's imagination or are used fictitiously. Any resemblance to actual events, locales, or persons, living or dead, is entirely coincidental.

BrickHouse Books, Inc. 2020
306 Suffolk Road
Baltimore, MD 21218

Distributor: Itasca Books, Inc.

ISBN: 978-1-938144-76-9

Printed in the United States of America

To Alex, Andrew and Aron

Always had the feeling
It will all come tumbling down.

— *Living in a Ghost Town* by Mick Jagger and Keith Richards

Table of Contents

Foreword..11
Prologue..13

Part One: The Run-in
Sunday, April 12, to Wednesday, April 15

Chapter One: HUTTON..19
Chapter Two: CRAIG...43
Chapter Three: BARTON...71

Part Two: The Runaround
Thursday, April 16, to Sunday, April 19

Chapter One: JUDKIS..77
Chapter Two: ORR...107
Chapter Three: MARCONI..129

Part Three: The Rundown
Monday, April 20, to Friday, April 24

Chapter One: SIMON...137
Chapter Two: STONE..151
Chapter Three: ST. VITUS' DANCE....................................175

Epilogue..213
Acknowledgements..217

Foreword

The COVID-19 virus was identified in Wuhan, China, in December 2019. The first known deaths in the U.S. occurred in February 2020. The World Health Organization (WHO) declared a pandemic on March 11. By Sunday, April 12, the number of U.S. deaths from COVID-19 reached 20,646. Worldwide, there were 1.8 million confirmed cases and over 100,000 deaths by that day.

The worst was yet to come.

Prologue

Sunday, April 12

BY 3 P.M., the rain had stopped and the sun appeared behind a thin veneer of white clouds. A cold front was moving into the Washington metropolitan area with more rain forecast behind it. Cherry trees and azaleas were in bloom, purple ajugas were sprouting, and oak trees prepared to unfurl new leaves from barren branches. Everywhere in sight, spring was bursting out.

No one seemed to notice or care. Throughout the metro area, people were sheltering in place as part of a nationwide effort to dampen the spread of the novel coronavirus. Earlier in the week, families had celebrated Passover on Skype. Today, Easter Sunday, Christian churches stood empty. Colorful spring hats and flowery dresses remained in boxes and on hangers. Many people were grateful simply to have food on the table. Easter dinner was punctuated by prayers for doctors, nurses, and emergency medical teams, police and firefighters, grocery store clerks, trash collectors, and airport workers, all of whom were saving lives and propping up a sagging economy.

Yesterday, Jane Hutton drove to Mount Vernon for a cardboard box filled with fruits and vegetables. She had called the produce company in advance and paid by credit card. Then she waited in line in her car in a church parking lot. She gave her name to a man wearing a mask and gloves who placed the box in the trunk of her SUV. This morning, the meat she ordered from a local charcuterie was delivered to her door. Tonight, she planned a grand meal for one, replete with candles and a glass of wine.

Some people disliked the new reality of sheltering in place, but Hutton enjoyed the respite. As the attorney in charge of the civil division of the U.S. Attorney's office, her professional life was chaotic, consuming, and confrontational. Her personal life was a mirror reflection. She liked maintaining distance from people without the need for excuses or appearing to be rude, particularly after today's fiasco. Perhaps there was a silver lining even in a pandemic, she thought.

Hutton had just returned to her townhome near Slaters Lane in the north end of Old Town Alexandria. She had been out for a run along the George Washington Parkway. Her bright red hair was captured in a ponytail and her elongated neck glistened with perspiration. Her clothes were drenched from the unexpected cloudburst. She went around to the back of the house, anxious to get inside and take a hot shower. The patio door was unlocked, the way she left it when she departed for her run. She slid the door open, took off her protective mask, and removed her sweatshirt.

The front doorbell rang.

What now? People were supposed to be home observing the guidance about six feet of separation, but that obviously was not happening today. She ran upstairs, past the kitchen. There was a potted plant on the counter. She went to the foyer, put the mask on a console table in front of a gilded mirror, and looked through the peep hole in the front door. She was not entirely surprised to see the person who stood outside. "I thought you'd be back," she said, opening the door.

The door swung inward. Two fast steps. The visitor moved forward quickly and Hutton moved back with equal urgency. Words of anger and betrayal were exchanged. Then a push. The sweatshirt in her hand acted as a buffer. Hutton held it between them like an airbag during a collision. A sharp pain. More sharp pains. She looked down. Blood was seeping through the nylon fibers of the shirt.

"What?" Her voice was frail. She was in a state of shock. Both her hands clutched the sweatshirt. Blood dripped on the wood floor and the Persian rug that adorned the foyer. She reached out one hand to grasp the door frame leading to the kitchen. The hand was dripping blood. Then she fell backwards and landed on the kitchen's tile floor. Blood quickly oozed into the grout between the tiles. She called out "Tricia," the name she had given her virtual personal assistant. In a nearly inaudible voice, she whispered, "Get help. Call 911."

The attacker stopped and glanced around quickly for the device that sat on a kitchen counter. No colorful lights danced around the rim. The attacker grabbed the sweatshirt from Hutton's feeble grasp and pushed it into her mouth. Hutton tried to speak but only muffled sounds emerged, and blood seeped out around the corners of her mouth. The assailant reached over her body and yanked the device's plug out of the wall, then put the machine into a bag. An item was removed, an imprint was made. A quick search was conducted for Hutton's phone, which was also placed in the bag. A second later the assailant fled downstairs through the sliding glass door, stopped for an instant at the edge of the patio, and disappeared down an alley between rows of townhouses.

Hutton pulled the sweatshirt out of her mouth. She spit out the blood that was choking her. She had been struck multiple times, but most of the wounds felt like bug stings compared to the pain in her stomach. She faded in and out of consciousness.

If she remained in the kitchen, she knew that she would die. No one would check on her tonight. The earliest would be tomorrow, and by then it would be too late. She had to will herself to the front door. If she remembered correctly, the door had not closed. If she could crawl across the tile floor and the wooden foyer, she could pry open the door with her bloody fingers. If she could do that, she could throw a hand over the threshold like a buoy being thrown into the water. Hopefully, someone would see it.

She turned on her side and began pulling herself toward the foyer. Her hands, wet with blood, slipped on the tile. Inch by inch she lurched closer to the door. She stopped and rested her cheek on the cold tile. The pain was excruciating. She let out a deep moan. The front door seemed so distant.

Part One

The Run-in
Sunday, April 12, to Wednesday, April 15

…Each new morn
New widows howl, new orphans cry, new sorrows
Strike heaven on the face…

> – Shakespeare
> Macbeth, act 4, scene 3

Chapter One: HUTTON

ELMO KATZ sat in front of the television watching the cable news channel. So much had happened in so short a time. People were reeling and disoriented. It was hard to believe that the State of the Union address was only six weeks ago. The memorial service for Kobe Bryant. When had that been? And it was only two months since Kansas City stormed back to win the Super Bowl. One sports commentator wrote it was a good thing the 49ers blew that fourth quarter lead. If a victory parade had been held in San Francisco, it would have coincided with the coronavirus peaking in Northern California and caused the illness to spread faster than it had, the commentator wrote. Everything seemed tinged by bitter irony as the country and the world battled a pandemic.

The phone rang. In the past three weeks, he had heard from high school, college, and law school friends, as well as colleagues and members of the law enforcement community. Everyone was checking up on loved ones and friends. This time it was Alexandria Detective Sherry Stone on the other end of the phone. "Good to hear from you," he said. "How are things in your world? I'm adjusting and acclimating, but it's weird." As the U.S. Attorney for the Eastern District of Virginia, he was dealing with shuttered courtrooms, postponed court dockets, disbanded grand juries, and prisons releasing convicts to minimize spread of the coronavirus.

"This isn't a social call." Stone's voice was flat. "It's about Jane Hutton."

"What about Jane?" He had just spoken with her on a video conference call two days ago.

"As we speak, she's being flown to Baltimore for emergency surgery."

Katz was incredulous. "The coronavirus?"

"I wish," Stone answered. The words sent a chill down his spine. *I wish.* The novel coronavirus was everyone's worst nightmare. It had shut down the world and indiscriminately killed people unprepared for the invasion of a foreign virus. Everyone dreaded getting it. While much was still being learned, the virus reportedly made a person's immunological system go haywire and blocked oxygen from secreting through the lungs into the blood system, thereby depriving vital organs of their lifeblood and resulting in catastrophic consequences or death.

"What are you talking about?" he asked.

"She was brutally stabbed in her home. It's a bloodbath. There's a stream of blood across the main floor of her townhouse. If some cop from the Sharon Tate murder walked in this afternoon, he'd have a bad case of déjà vu."

"I'm…"

"Yeah, I know. The good news is she's alive, and damn lucky to be, though it's doubtful she's going to pull through. Somehow, she managed to pull herself from the kitchen to the front door, a good 20 feet. The trail looks like someone mopped the floor with her blood. It's pretty gross.

"Fortunately, she got to the doorway and somehow opened it. There was a guy out walking his dog and he saw her. He called it in. I rushed over right away. I'll be honest and tell you that I thought she was a goner when I first saw her. Anyway, I wanted you to know about it before we go public."

"I'll come right over," he said.

"Don't." She lowered her voice. "Half of the people here have been to hospitals, nursing homes, and public facilities in the past two weeks. If they'd been tested before they reported to work today, a lot of them would be showing positive results for the coronavirus. In addition to the risk of getting the virus by coming here now, there's nothing for you to do."

"She's being transported by helicopter to Johns Hopkins Hospital. The best thing you can do is hold off until tomorrow. If I'd known you were going to invite yourself over, I would not have called you. This place is a major crime scene and a lot of people are crawling around. Let the tech guys do their job. Drop by in the morning. They'll be finished by then. You can survey the scene at that time. There is simply no reason for you to come now."

"I appreciate you looking out for me," Katz said. "I'll be there in 10 minutes."

He slipped his bare feet into a pair of topsiders and threw on a light windbreaker over a blue T-shirt. He wore khaki shorts and didn't see any need to change into a pair of pants. As he matted down his hair in front of the hallway mirror, the reflection showed a tall, lanky man with steel wool hair graying at the temples, olive skin, and dark, piercing eyes. He ran an open palm over the stubble on his cheek. He had not shaved in three days.

Admiring yourself?" asked Abby Snowe, slim and blonde, who appeared around the corner. She wrapped an arm around his waist. Following a series of starts and stops that began a decade ago when he was a young city prosecutor and she was a newly hired probation officer, their relationship had blossomed into a full-fledged romance. She was dressed in a cotton top and yoga pants. "Where are you off to?"

"Sherry Stone called. Someone tried to kill Jane Hutton earlier today. She's being transported by helicopter to the ICU at Johns Hopkins."

Snowe separated from him and crossed her arms over her chest. "Oh, my God!" She said. "Who would do a thing like that to her?" Her eyes welled with tears. "What are you going to do? Are you going to drive up to be with her?"

Katz paused. "I was planning to drive over to her place, but it actually makes more sense to go to the hospital, doesn't it?" Snowe wiped her eyes and said nothing, allowing him to weigh the pros and cons. "She doesn't have any family, except her mother, Tricia, who's in her late 60s or early 70s. If something happens to Jane, I want to be there."

Snowe opened the closet door. "Under normal circumstances, I'd try to discourage you from driving to a hospital in the middle of a pandemic," she said. "But Jane was one of your top people and I know how much you care about your staff." She pulled out an umbrella and a thin wool scarf. "You'll need this for the rain, which is pretty fierce. And you should wear this mask at Hutton's place and in the hospital, assuming you're going to both places."

An instant later, he raced through the rain to his car. He clicked the fob, hopped inside, closed the umbrella, and slammed the door. He threw the umbrella in the backseat. The scarf hung loosely around his neck. He started the car and looked at the dashboard. The gas tank was full. He had only driven about ten miles in the past week and that was only to and from the grocery store. The digital clock on the dash read 4:15.

He took a series of left and right turns at intersections through Old Town from his home on Harvard Street to Hutton's place near Slaters Lane. The sky and the road were black. Streets and sidewalks were deserted. Even in the steady rain, he felt as though he inhabited a ghost town. Everywhere he went — on those occasions when he drove at all — he witnessed hollowed out communities. Alexandria, Washington D.C., Richmond, and Baltimore were all empty. People had heeded the warnings and stayed indoors hoping the Angel of Death would pass by their door. It was too ugly to contemplate catching the virus. You'd end up on a ventilator pumping oxygen through your lungs to prevent your vital organs from shutting down.

As he drove toward Hutton's home, he pulled up Mike "Mac" McCarthy's phone number on the car's Bluetooth system. McCarthy helped Katz set up shop in 2017 when Katz was confirmed as U.S. Attorney for the Eastern District of Virginia. McCarthy came from the congressional office of Senator Abraham Lowenstein, who became Katz's benefactor following Katz's impressive handling of the Daingerfield Island murder case. McCarthy served as deputy of the criminal division. He and Hutton were equals in the office, Katz's two right hands. He was 40, with roguish auburn hair, piercing blue eyes, and strong Gaelic features.

"Jane Hutton's been brutally attacked," Katz said when McCarthy answered his phone. "I'm headed to her place now."

"Poor thing," McCarthy replied. "So much going right for her. The job, everything. I'm still processing it." He said he'd learned about it on the news a half hour ago.

Katz pulled up to Hutton's place. "Jane's loss is going to have a devastating impact on the office, particularly with people already upset over the coronavirus," he said. Although no one in the office had yet contracted the virus, everyone was fearful as it spread through the D.C. metropolitan area. Several attorneys in the office were married to nurses, doctors and emergency medical technicians who were on the front line in the battle against the virus and were worried the virus might find its way into their homes. "I'll call you back later," Katz said and hung up. He reached for the umbrella, raised the scarf so it covered his face, and exited the car.

Uniforms in long black raincoats and boots had set up a tarp on Hutton's lawn outside the front door of her townhouse. After showing his ID, Katz received a pair of gloves and slip-on foot coverings. He put on the gloves and pulled the coverings over his topsiders. He looked at the lock on the front door, stepped inside carefully and surveyed the scene.

He noticed the protective mask on the console table pushed to a corner of the foyer. Ironic, he thought to himself. Hutton had undoubtedly worn a mask outdoors as a layer of protection against an unseen virus. Yet she had suffered a life-threatening injury from a human predator when she opened the front door.

A huge smear of blood extended from the kitchen to the front door. Blood had seeped through the wood in the foyer and formed a dark crimson stain. The Persian rug had dark spots on it. And there was a puddle of blood on the tile in the kitchen.

"Quite a mess," said Stone as she greeted him. She wore a black leather jacket and black pants. A white mask wrapped over the lower half of her face accentuated her brown skin and dark inscrutable eyes. Her burnt orange hair was shaved on the sides and full on top. Like Katz, she wore blue latex gloves and disposable blue shoe covers. "Want a tour?"

"I'm not staying," he said. "I'm heading up to Baltimore to check on Jane's condition. I just wanted to stop by and thank you for contacting me. Have you been able to notify the family? When I say family, I mean her mother. That's all the family she's got."

"Not yet."

"Okay." He looked around. He remembered Stone saying it didn't make any sense for him to drop by tonight. She was right. Several technicians were working the scene. "How long ago was she transported to Baltimore?" he asked.

"In the last 15 minutes," Stone said, pulling down her protective mask. "The chopper was lifting off as I was literally dialing your number." She shook her head. "You should have seen her. There was only a flicker of fire inside her. She may die before they land in Baltimore."

He drew his thumb across his cheek. It felt like sandpaper. "Listen," he said, "I know the police department is stretched thin with a lot of people sick and others helping at the Alexandria Hospital and elsewhere. Let me know if my people can help. I can shift around duties and responsibilities, particularly with everyone in my office teleworking at the present time. I'd love to put Santana and a few of the others on the case. They can help you. It's important to me."

"Okay," she said. "I'll talk to the chief and call you back. It's a little unusual for us to accept help from the U.S. Attorney's office with an investigation but these are unusual times. We may need all the help we can get."

Katz returned to his car. As he did so, a television truck pulled up. There was only one person in it. That person would shoot film through the window of the van and send it to the station. A reporter would cover the story from her home. No one was going to set up a tent with lights tonight. Like everything else, the news was being served *a la carte*. He started the engine, and minutes later he was headed to the hospital via the Baltimore-Washington Parkway.

Conducting an investigation in the midst of the coronavirus pandemic would be challenging, particularly the early stages, he reasoned. He wondered how the process of collecting and storing evidence and of interviewing witnesses was going to be affected. If Hutton died, would the medical examiner find time to conduct the autopsy while also conducting work to better understand the virus? Would clues be overlooked?

He had investigators, researchers, and prosecutors who could assist. Hutton was one of his people. Quick and decisive action would be needed to capture the person reasonable for attacking her before the coronavirus made it difficult to solve the crime.

Across the Potomac, the lights of downtown Washington D.C. shone brightly. Residential dwellings were filled with anxious occupants while office buildings stood vacant like the old R.F.K. football stadium he saw to his left. The signs for the Baltimore Washington Parkway were barely visible in the rain. He signaled and shifted onto the parkway. It was a route with which he was familiar. He always had to look to the left to be sure he could merge into the traffic driving up from D.C. But not tonight. The roadway was deserted. There was no one behind, alongside, or in front of him. No one was coming down the opposite direction on the parkway. It was as though he was driving in a city that had just suffered a nuclear attack. In a way, he thought to himself, he was.

A few minutes later the car phone jangled. He had been ignoring the frequent bursts of calls, but seeing it was Stone he answered this time.

"I checked with the chief," she said. "To say we're stretched thin is an understatement. I'll accept whatever resources you can provide."

He suspected she had pulled some strings. "Thanks, Sherry," he said. "I don't know the degree to which you're doing this because you know how badly I want to help, but I appreciate it. You're a friend."

"Who do you have in mind for the case?" she asked.

Katz drove along the parkway at 80 miles an hour. He knew that speed was unsafe in the best of conditions and bordered on recklessness given the increasing volume of rain. But traffic was nonexistent, and no officer wanted to risk contracting the virus by stopping him to write a speeding ticket. The only thing he was worried about was hydroplaning. "I'd put three of my best people on it," he replied. "Mac McCarthy, Mai Lin, and, of course, Curtis."

"I'm okay with the first two," she replied, having previously worked with both Lin and McCarthy. "As for Curtis, I'm not so sure." They both laughed. Curtis Santana was her live-in lover. "Actually, Mo, I couldn't think of a better threesome," she continued. "They're smart, dedicated, and discreet. I'll also get David involved," she said, referring to David Reese, Lin's husband, who was interning at the Alexandria Police Department as he finished law school. "His semester's probably blown to shit already, so he should have the time when he and Mai aren't tending to their baby." Their son was about five months old.

"I have a daily teleconference scheduled with them tomorrow morning," Katz said. "We'll go over the case then. If you can let Curtis know, I'll call Mac and Lin."

"Be careful tonight," Stone said. "The rain is coming down pretty heavy and people drive along that road like it's a five-lane interstate, with the exception of a stretch where everybody knows a speed camera is located." Katz sighed; he had blown through it. "And be careful when you get to the hospital. The coronavirus is the real deal."

"Will do," he said, tucking his chin into the fold of the scarf that Snowe had given him.

He hung up and called McCarthy. "I'm on my way to Baltimore

now," he said. The wipers swept across the windshield at high speed, pushing aside buckets of rain that made it difficult to clearly see the roadway. "We're in business. I've offered our assistance to Sherry Stone and she graciously accepted it."

"Great," McCarthy replied. "If we simply keep initial leads from growing cold, we'll perform a valuable service."

Katz uttered his concurrence. Then he added: "Before I forget, I want to get everyone on a video call first thing tomorrow morning. Can you line that up? People are going to hear about it tonight and they're going to freak out. My phone's been beeping nonstop but I'm not going to take any of the calls. I want an all-hands. We can hold out hope together."

"I'll set it up for 9," he said. "Now, what can you tell me about the crime scene? What did you see? Any clues to work on tonight?"

"I only did a cursory inspection," Katz said. "There did not appear to be any forced entry because there was no evidence that the front door was damaged. The assault itself appeared to be confined to the foyer and the kitchen, which is in the front of the house, directly next to the hallway. There is blood everywhere. No blood in other rooms, from what I could see, but I was only in those two rooms. It's hard to say whether the altercation started in the kitchen or in the foyer. Somehow, Jane dragged herself to the front door and somehow managed to pull her body over the threshold sufficient for a passerby to see it. Nothing was disturbed in either of those two rooms. So there was no fight or robbery or anything like that."

"Prints?"

"Didn't see any."

"Murder weapon?"

"Had to be a knife, given the amount of blood at the scene, but I didn't ask and Sherry didn't say anything about recovering a weapon at the scene." Katz reflected. "Maybe it'll be discovered when they search the house and the surrounding area. It's impossible to say whether the assailant came to the house with the intent of killing her or whether there was an altercation and someone grabbed a knife."

"Premeditated or heat of passion," McCarthy said.

Only a lawyer would be thinking about defenses at an early stage, Katz thought to himself.

A knock at the front door. Hutton opened it. She recognized the assailant. While she was surprised, there was no reason to be alarmed. It was the middle of the afternoon on Easter Sunday. Yet, the streets were deserted. Everyone was hunkered down in their homes because of the coronavirus. No one drove or walked by the house. There was an eerie calm. If someone wanted to enter undetected, this was the time. The front door closed. Harsh, accusatory words were exchanged. Suddenly a knife was waved in the air. The parties tussled. Hutton was stabbed. The other party panicked and fled from the house.

McCarthy shook his head. "It's easy to dream up scenarios that might have unfolded," he said. "I find myself doing that sort of thing all the time. But I doubt Hutton brought the knife to the fight, so to speak. It sounds like someone came to the door and attacked her when she answered it."

"Yeah, I know," Katz said. "You have to be careful when you concoct scenarios in your head. If you draw inferences too quickly, you can overlook things."

"Of course," McCarthy said. "This reminds me of a 2003 case in Old Town involving Nancy Dunning, the wife of the local sheriff at the time. She opened the door to her home and was shot to death. It took over a decade before they arrested and prosecuted someone for the murder."

"I vaguely remember hearing about that case," said Katz. "So you think this case is similar? What areas do you think we need to study? Where would you like to devote your energies?"

"Off the top of my head, I say we study Jane's personal contacts. We start with the premise that she was killed by someone who knew her. There was no forced entry. She opened the door knowing who was on the other side. She was not afraid to open the door. We should look at family members. We need to know if she had any enemies at work, in the community, or at her old firm, including clients and opposing counsel. If we're lucky, we might flush out the assailant in a few days."

"That sounds about right," Katz said. "Except I'm not so sure she necessarily knew the other party. People open their doors without thinking all of the time. That case you just mentioned. Dunning. Did she know the person who was finally arrested for her murder?"

"No."

"That supports my argument."

"Not these days, Mo," McCarthy cautioned. "We're living in the Age of the Coronavirus. Fear of the virus flies in the face of the instinct to open the door without thinking. In fact, to me, the absence of forced entry suggests not only that she knew the person on the other side but that the person who knocked was someone she trusted enough to believe they were not carrying the virus. The person was a known quantity. She had some knowledge of that person's recent movements. Think about it."

"You might have a point," Katz conceded.

"If you want, I can begin by reviewing her current cases in the office," McCarthy said. "She's only been with us for a short while so there won't be a lot there. I can do that review and then help out in the other areas. By the way, what's her medical status? They didn't really provide any details on the news."

"I'll find out when I get to the hospital," Katz said. "Stone didn't sound optimistic. In fact, she was ready to place odds on whether she'd die in the helicopter before she gets to Johns Hopkins. If Jane dies, it's going to be hard to track down the killer in this climate. There's neither the people nor the inclination to devote the resources needed to solving a malicious assault right now. If there was ever a moment when you could get away with a crime, this is it."

29

"We can narrow the list of suspects to a handful of people within a couple of days," McCarthy said. "I'll start doing some work online tonight. These crimes are always committed by family members or close friends." He remembered the Dunning case. "Almost always," he added. "And I'll schedule a meeting for the entire staff for first thing tomorrow morning."

Katz thanked his deputy and called Lin. David Reese answered the phone. "Mai's putting the baby to bed," he said. "We heard the news about Jane Hutton. Let me have her call you right back."

As promised, when his phone dinged a few minutes later it was Mai Lin. He could picture her: cherubic smile, warm eyes, and long, dark flowing hair. "Is it true, Mo?" she asked. "Has Jane been injured? Have they arrested any suspects? Are there any witnesses? Who's investigating? Is Sherry assigned to the case? Can I help? What's Jane's prognosis? Where is she now?" She always had questions, which was the reason she was the chief research assistant in the office. Every attorney wanted her assigned to their case.

"She was attacked in her home," Katz said. "No one's been arrested. There are no suspects at this time. Sherry Stone is handling the case and she's consented for us to help for a few days. I'd like you to work alongside Mac and Curtis Santana."

"I'm eager to assist any way I can," she replied.

"We'll figure out assignments tomorrow, after we have a video conference with the entire staff to discuss Jane's condition," Katz said. "And, by the way, when and how did you hear about it?"

"It was on the five o'clock news. At first, they didn't release a name. They only said it was an attorney. Then they announced it was her. I was listening to WAMU. It was the local headlines following the national news at the top of the hour. By the way, all the news is pretty bad. More people are testing positive and dying from COVID-19. The epicenter's been in New York but it's beginning to look as though it might be migrating down to our area."

Katz thought of Lin and Reese and their baby boy. "Fortunately," he said, "it doesn't seem to attack young people. You need to take normal precautions, but you don't have to worry about it like older people."

"How are your parents? They live outside of the city, don't they?"

"They do and thanks for asking," he said. "They're fine," he explained, although he had not contacted them in years. The last time he even thought about seeing them was in 2017 while returning from former U.S. Attorney Helen O. Douglas's funeral in Massachusetts. He was on the Taconic State Parkway and planned to stop at their home in the Hudson Valley, but veered away from the exit ramp at the last second.

"I appreciate your taking the time to call me," Lin said. "I looked up to Jane. She was a role model for me and other women in the office. I hope she survives. And I'm honored to work with you to try to find her assailant."

The incessant noise from the phone continued to interrupt his thoughts, but Katz did not answer any of the calls. He knew that other attorneys and staff in the office, judges, attorneys, and friends were inquiring about Hutton's condition. He had spoken to the people with whom he needed to share information. Everyone else could wait.

As he drove by Thurgood Marshall BWI Airport, he dialed a number he knew by heart. He might not know any of the phone numbers of his current friends and colleagues, but some phone numbers were emblazoned in his memory.

"Hello."

"Pops, it's Mo."

How long ago had it been? A decade? Maybe longer. His relationship with his parents was always strained, but the last conversation with his father was particularly ugly. The love child born of an interracial relationship between Myron Katz and Denise Wells, two students at the University of Chicago in the late '70s, Katz struggled for years with his identity.

31

"Throughout my life, you avoided creating ties and bonds for our family," he accused his father. *"You don't want us to identify with any group, or so you say. The result is we don't identify with anyone. I'm not affiliated with your side of the family or with mom's side. I'm unmoored and untethered. I'm alienated by design. My education, my neighborhood, my religion, everything. I never forged an identity as a Jew or as a Protestant, and it's always been unclear if I'm black or white. Neither side rejects me but neither side accepts me either. Everyone regards me with suspicion. As a result, all my relationships are superficial. I exist on the surface. My whole life has been as a sole survivor. I hold you responsible for all of it."*

"How are you, son?" The voice was warm and tender, almost mournful. There was no sense of anger or resentment. "It's been a long time."

Katz struggled for words. Should he address their final conversation and his bitter parting words? Had his father's memory of that conversation faded or was it as fresh as it was in his mind? He stuttered and stammered. Then the emotions flowed.

"I'm sorry about that conversation, Pops. I shouldn't have said some of those things. I was in a bad place. I blamed you for things I did to myself." He took a deep breath and continued. "I've since discovered I'm a composite of rich and vibrant heritages. You and mom gave me your strengths. I just didn't see it that way at the time.

"You don't have to apologize," Myron Katz said. "I'll be candid with you. I'm a guy who never fit in. So I cut ties. I made choices that placed me outside the mainstream. I created cultural fault lines. You just fell into them.

"Those fissures have healed because the times have changed. People embrace diversity today. It wasn't always that way. I never wanted you to get hurt. In trying to protect you, I isolated you and that hurt you more than if I'd done nothing. So don't say you're sorry. I'm the one who's sorry."

Katz was grateful to hear his father's explanation. In the past, their talks were strained. Tonight was different. Perhaps they had both conducted countless imaginary conversations with one another to get to this place. Katz had certainly done so. He gripped the steering wheel tightly and realized his palms were sweating. "I tried to visit you and mom a couple of times, but I never had the courage to do it," he said. "Maybe I can drive up and visit in a couple of weeks? Is Mom there?"

"Your Mom is in the hospital, son."

Katz was stunned. He held his breath and hoped his father was going to say that Mom was in the hospital for routine surgery. But he knew elective surgeries had been postponed until the pandemic subsided.

"She's got a bad cough," he said. "We were down in Westchester County last month, the weekend of March 14th. Not a good time as it turned out. The virus was circulated all over the place at that time.

"Everyone's talking about the need for more ventilators, more ventilators. As far as I'm concerned, you're already counted among the dead if you get hooked up to one of those things. No, she's not on a ventilator. She's resting comfortably."

"Have you seen her? Where is she?"

"I haven't seen her. They won't let me in. I've got an underlying condition, if you haven't forgotten. Diabetes. She's at Mt. Sinai. She's okay. She's going to be okay."

"Are *you* okay?"

He paused. "Yeah, son. I'm fine. Your mother and I had a wonderful life. I still remember falling in love with her in Chicago." Katz's name — Elmo — was inspired by the L, the 'elevated' rapid transit system that served as his parents' method of transportation when they were students at the University of Chicago, and Motown Records, the recording company whose songs and melodies by Smokey, Diana, and Marvin buoyed their romance. L-Mo.

"I always marched to my own drummer. It might have caused problems for you growing up. It might have created discord in our relationship. It certainly created friction with her family, as well as mine. But I have no regrets. And it's what keeps me going now. So I'm doin' just fine."

"Will you keep me informed of how she's doing?"

"Sure," he said. "Send me your email and I'll write you daily updates. By the way, your mother and I have been following your career. Congratulations on being named U.S. Attorney. I read how Abe Lowenstein championed your nomination and shepherded your confirmation. He's a good man. Last of a dying breed. Independent minded, honest. Keep doin' good, son. Your mother and I are very proud of you."

Katz's lips trembled. His cheeks turned crimson. He swallowed hard. "Yeah," he said. "Thanks." When he hung up the phone, he felt disoriented. He wondered what had compelled him to place the call in the first place. Was it Lin's comment or was it the coronavirus? Maybe he was acutely aware of the fragility of life, he thought.

Until now, the 'defining' moment of his life was 9/11. He had just started college when the planes hit the World Trade Center. It had made a lasting impression on him and drove him into public service.

The coronavirus made the crashing of airplanes by terrorists in New York, Washington, and a field in Shanksville, Pennsylvania, appear insignificant by comparison. COVID-19 was not going to be a singular event followed by a lengthy recovery period. This was a rolling disaster, the Four Horsemen of the Apocalypse riding across America from San Francisco and Los Angeles to New York and then stopping everyplace in between. "Recovery" did not mean a return to the way things had been before. He was not sure what the future held, but he knew that the uncertainty of the future compelled him to reach out to his father and make amends for the past.

*

KATZ RACED along the BW Parkway. As he entered

Baltimore, he tapped his map app and requested the Johns Hopkins Hospital. He followed the directions and arrived at the center in 20 minutes. He located a parking space, pulled up the scarf over his face, and, opening the umbrella, dashed into the night. He avoided the emergency entrance and found a side entrance that was not intended for access by the public.

"You can't enter this way," a guard announced. Katz turned. She was armed and wearing a blue shirt with a yellow badge sown over her breast pocket. She wore a white mask over her nose and mouth. She sounded like a recording; she must have been announcing the same warning all day long as people tried to avoid the emergency room entrance to sneak inside to seek medical assistance or visit loved ones.

Katz flashed his badge. "Mo Katz, U.S. Attorney for the Eastern District of Virginia," he said. "One of my two deputy U.S. Attorneys arrived here a short while ago. She is the victim of a stabbing in Alexandria. I need to see her."

Without hesitation, the officer escorted him down the lobby to an information center. From there, he was taken in an elevator to an upper floor and told to wait outside an operating room. He sat alone in a plastic chair along a wall of windows staring out at the black night. Rain pounded against the window.

Finally, one of the members of the surgical team found him an hour later. "She's probably not going to make it through the night," said the surgeon. "She's barely hanging on. She's suffered a serious abdominal stab wound and lost a considerable amount of blood. But for the miraculous work performed by the medical evacuation team, she'd be dead."

Katz gulped. "She's a fighter. She doesn't give up." He digested what the surgeon had told him. "If she makes it through the night, what are her chances going forward?"

The surgeon was dressed in blue scrubs, including a V-neck top, mask, and cap. He had deep circles under his eyes. He was thin and slightly taller than Katz, probably 6 foot 2 inches in height. Despite the fact he had to be insanely busy, he gave the impression that he was not in a hurry to finish the conversation and get back to work. Katz attributed it to a good bedside manner.

"Each day she pulls through enhances the prospects of recovery," he said. "It's too soon to tell whether the loss of blood has caused any permanent damage. Fortunately, the other punctures were surface lacerations inflicted without a lot of force. The serious wound damaged her abdominal aorta and her left kidney lobe.

"I hope you aren't planning to see her tonight, because, if you are, you're out of luck. She's heavily sedated. It'll be at least three to four days before we know whether she's going to live or die. If she survives, you can visit her in about ten days. Even then, you're going to have to be tested for the coronavirus before you are allowed into her room."

Katz thanked the doctor. He said he'd contact her next of kin in the morning and provide a status of her condition. The surgeon never inquired about the circumstances surrounding the attack, and Katz didn't volunteer any details. Despite the fact that their encounter was brief, Katz picked up one valuable piece of information, namely that all but one of the wounds inflicted by the assailant were superficial.

He departed the hospital by the same route he used to enter. There was a brief respite from the rain. He walked down the street with the umbrella by his side and found a park bench under a streetlamp. He lowered the scarf from his face. He wiped the water from the bench but still the rainwater penetrated the seat of his khaki shorts when he sat down. The street was black and glossy. He smelled fresh dirt and mulch. A landscaping crew must have been here in the past day or so.

He thought about the fragility of life. Things could turn on a dime. Just a couple of months ago, they were playing the Super Bowl in Miami and conducting an impeachment trial in the U.S. Senate. Now all professional sports were cancelled, members of Congress were hunkered down in their districts, and the Supreme Court was hearing cases by teleconference. The stock market, which had been on an upward trajectory, was now a veritable roller coaster, trending in who knew which direction. And look at what had happened to his family and his office. His mother was hospitalized and his father was unable to comfort her. One of his two principal deputies was fighting for her life. And everyone in his office was working remotely to stave off the spread of a pandemic.

The security guard he had encountered in the hospital suddenly appeared along the sidewalk. She walked up to him and asked, "You Mo Katz, the defense attorney?" Katz nodded. "You represented my nephew, Tony Fortune. Actually, you represented him a lot of times. He showed me a picture of you and him together." She laughed. She and Katz both knew it was a newspaper photo following one of Fortune's many acquittals. "Our entire family is indebted to you. You done a lot of good for people regardless of what they did or who they was. You musta been brought up the right way."

Katz got up from the bench. They bumped elbows. She smiled and bid farewell, going back up the sidewalk toward the hospital.

The rain started as Katz headed to the car, but he didn't quicken his pace or raise the umbrella. He thought about a line from "Hamilton." *The world turned upside down.* He started to sing it as he walked through the rain.

On the drive home, he thought about Hutton. She risked her professional career to do the right thing in the case in which they had been adversaries. It would have been actionable if anyone could prove he offered her a job as a quid pro quo for her management of that case. But they both knew the truth, even if no one else could prove it.

A deluge began. The rain remained heavy all the way back to Alexandria. It seemed to have taken forever to get to the hospital, but he was back home before he knew it.

Snowe got out of bed and came downstairs when she heard him

enter their townhouse. He was rummaging through the refrigerator, which was half empty. Some items — such as almond milk and meat — were hard to find, but the refrigerator was well stocked with eggs and two freshly opened jars of peanut butter. He wondered whether there was enough bread to make a peanut butter sandwich.

They embraced. "First," he said, "Jane's alive. Her abdominal aorta and left kidney were cut or damaged. She lost a lot of blood and it's questionable whether she'll make it. But she's alive."

She exhaled and nodded her head. "It's a good thing you went to see her. If she died, you'd never forgive yourself."

"Second," he continued. "I spoke to my Pops."

"You called your parents?" She tightened her embrace. She knew about the strained relationship. She often counseled Katz that he should be grateful for the independence that his parents provided to him. She believed it was the source of his special gift of being able to connect with people. "Your empathy comes from your parents," she was fond of saying.

"Mom's been hospitalized at Mt. Sinai."

She looked him in the eyes. Her arms were still wrapped around him. "She has COVID-19?"

"Yeah, but she's not on a ventilator. I have no idea what will happen next. Pops has diabetes so he isn't going to visit her."

She broke the embrace and stood in the center of the room as though she was going to break out in dance. "I'm sorry about your mother but I am so proud of you. What possessed you to contact them?" As she said it, she knew. It was the virus. Maybe it was also a premonition that something was wrong and that he needed to put aside past animus and reach out to them. "Your mother will survive. You will be reunited with her. And," she turned to the refrigerator, "I recommend the jar with the nuts. It's delicious. Plus I went to the bakery today. We have plenty of bread."

*

REAGAN NATIONAL Airport registered 2.5 inches of rain overnight. The weather in the metro area on Monday was unsettled. Tornadoes were predicted in Montgomery County while the sun was shining in Alexandria. Tweets circulated under the heading #FireFauci. The annual Easter egg roll at the White House was cancelled. And it was the anniversary of the heroic return of Apollo 13.

Katz returned to Hutton's townhome near Slaters Lane before 8 a.m. He'd gotten four hours of sleep. He hadn't shaved or showered. The entrance to the residence was covered in yellow tape. Stone was waiting for him on the front stoop, wearing a mask. She opened the pocket of her pants and handed him a mask in a plastic covering. "Put it on," she said. She also had a pair of plastic bags for him to slip over his shoes and a pair of gloves. "It's still a mess," she explained. "They're not going to finish the forensics until later today."

Inside, Katz observed the stream of blood from the front door to the kitchen tile. He also studied the front door. The bottom corner was covered with dry blood. "She dragged herself from the kitchen," Stone explained. "The door must have remained open after the visitor entered. There's no blood on the handle or doorknob, only on the edge down there." She pointed to the smudge. "If the door had been closed, she would be dead. She clearly lacked the strength to get on her knees to turn the doorknob and open the door. As fate had it, she must have remembered the door was left ajar and she forced herself to get in a position where a passerby would be able to see her."

"Do we know who called it in?"

"Some random guy walking a dog," she said. "He checks out. He was living down in Lexington. Moved back home when the pandemic first broke out. He was looking for a store to buy wine or beer. Nice kid. Fresh out of college. Says it's weird moving back home and that the 'rents are driving him crazy. He's got no discernible connection to Hutton. I interviewed him myself. He's not a suspect. Quite the contrary. He's the quintessential Good Samaritan."

Katz was satisfied and ruled out the Good Samaritan as a suspect.

They moved from the foyer to the kitchen. Specks of blood were all on the walls. A puddle of dried blood was on the tile floor. "Hutton was probably stabbed in the foyer as soon as she opened the door," Stone said. "She fell backwards onto the kitchen floor. The assailant must have assumed she had been killed and left."

Katz stood with his feet on two adjoining tiles and slowly turned around. "It's odd that the assailant left before finishing the job," he said. "Do you think it's possible that something spooked the attacker? Maybe there was somebody else here, or maybe the assailant thought there was. Or maybe there were two assailants, one ran off prematurely and the other one followed."

He got down on his haunches in front of the dried puddle of blood. "You stab someone in the stomach, clearly intending to kill them. They fall to the ground. You then get on top of them and finish the job, don't you?" He stood up. "Nothing else makes sense. If you leave before they're dead, they might recover. If that happens, you're going to be ID'd and spend the next 30 years of your life in jail." He walked over to the window and glanced outside. "Something happened."

Stone was dubious. "The other possibility is that the attacker was confident she was dead or beyond the point of recovery and left. It's hard to believe Hutton would be able to crawl to the door having lost so much blood. Also, it was a miracle the door was not closed. Finally, the chances of someone spotting her, calling for help, and getting her airlifted to a hospital is borderline unbelievable. They landed the helicopter on Slaters Lane, right over there." She pointed out the window. "A slight variation on the theme, a minute here or there, and she'd be dead. So I don't find it unusual that the assailant left. For all intents and purposes, the job was finished."

Katz shook his head. "Either way, we're going to catch the son of a bitch who did this, Stoner. We're gonna form a posse and we're gonna hunt him down."

"Like I said last night, I appreciate all the help you can give me," she said. "Curtis was already working on the case last night. I couldn't get him to bed."

Katz noticed a potted plant on the counter.

"I have no idea who brought that," Stone said. "Maybe she bought it or maybe someone gave it to her for Easter. It came from the hardware store down Washington Street over by Faccia Luna. We'll check it out." She didn't move all the while she stood in the kitchen. It never occurred to Katz that she was blocking his view.

"One other thing," she said. "We checked the cutlery. All of the knives are accounted for. So the murder weapon was brought into the house by another person. That person still has the murder weapon in their possession."

Chapter Two: CRAIG

KATZ RETURNED home, showered, and shaved. He turned on his laptop and joined the video call that McCarthy scheduled for 9. Attorneys and support staff from the Alexandria, Richmond and Norfolk branches of the U.S. Attorney's office participated, along with FBI investigators, contractors, military personnel, and Department of Justice and Homeland Security attorneys on detail. The screen of Katz's computer was like the reel of film with each frame depicting a different face. Some faces were pressed close to the lens and others were set back, displaying rooms in homes where makeshift offices had been established. Children's drawings, expensive artwork, china cabinets, closets, dressers, and other items were displayed in the rooms. Several participants wore Washington Nationals or Capitals caps. Almost everyone's hair was longer and disheveled. Several of the men, previously clean-shaven, were growing beards.

"It's nice to see everyone this morning," he began. "It's a tribute to Jane. As has been widely reported, she was attacked and brutally stabbed by an unknown assailant yesterday afternoon in her home. She is currently hospitalized in Baltimore in critical condition. She suffered tremendous blood loss and internal injuries. It's too soon to say whether she's going to pull through."

"Have you seen her?" The question was asked by one of the attorneys from Richmond. As she spoke, her image appeared on the screen.

"I drove up to Baltimore last night. As you can imagine, I wasn't able to see her. But I got her prognosis from the doctor. To be honest, it's not good. I've also visited the crime scene and spoke to the lead investigator. I haven't actually seen Jane since last Friday, but I've got a feel for how she's doing and of what happened to her."

There were a hundred questions that people wanted to ask, but the audience remained silent.

"I don't want to make this sound like a eulogy, but I want us to remember who Jane Hutton is and what she means to our office," Katz said. "Since she joined us as the deputy U.S. Attorney for the civil division about six months ago, she's done an outstanding job overseeing the civil docket. She's smart, popular, and highly motivated. Jane earned her B.A. at Amherst and she holds both a J.D. and an M.B.A. from Duke. She's an avid Blue Devil fan."

There were a smattering of hisses and applause. Many of the people on the video call hailed from Atlantic Coast Conference, Big East, and Big Ten schools. Katz contemplated asking who would have won the N.C.A.A. Tournament. But with all conference tournaments and March Madness cancelled, the call would have become chaotic and unruly with everyone shouting out the name of their alma mater. Instead, he stuck to the script he had sketched on a piece of paper beside him.

"When your mother is Tricia Barton, it might be difficult to come out from under the shadow of your celebrity parent and attain your own brand of success," Katz continued. He put a photo of them on the screen. It was like seeing Anderson Cooper and Gloria Vanderbilt or Janet Leigh and Jamie Lee Curtis. Except the two figures were identical: red hair, emerald eyes, and white marble skin. A few people gasped, but no one said anything. Katz continued, "But Jane Hutton succeeded beyond imagination. She became a partner at Stephens Babcock & Brazier in record time and defended some of the firm's biggest clients, including the Bank of Magellan, affectionately known as the BOM."

Several attorneys laughed. They remembered the office's successful prosecution against the bank last year under the supervision of McCarthy and Katz.

"Many of you remember the civil and criminal counts we filed against BOM for its role in laundering terrorist dollars that financed the death of several Marines," Katz said. "I met Jane Hutton while negotiating the settlement. I was impressed by her poise and professionalism. She could have pushed the case to trial but chose not to, primarily, I think, because it was in her client's best interest to avoid the bad publicity that would have resulted, to say nothing of the fact that she would have lost the case."

He could have added that she settled the case because she couldn't abide by her clients' misdeeds. But to say that would be like outing her. As everyone on the call knew, attorneys are never supposed to put their personal feelings ahead of those of their clients. If Katz had permitted his personal feelings to influence his courtroom strategy as a criminal defense attorney, he never would have been able to defend the felons for whom he consistently won acquittals.

"I saw something extraordinary in Jane when we met and I offered her a job shortly after the settlement," he continued. "I pride myself in the choices I make hiring attorneys and staff for this office, as evidenced by several of you on this call. You're all great attorneys — the best prosecutor's office in the federal government, bar none — but I never made a better choice than Jane Hutton."

He wasn't exaggerating by much. She might have been abrasive toward some of the line attorneys and she may have made decisions to pursue or drop cases with which others disagreed. But at this moment there was only room for praise.

"We are going to assist the Alexandria Police Department in the initial investigation of the case," Katz continued. "I'm going to ask a couple of people on our staff to assist me." Everyone knew it would consist of the inner circle he had brought with him from private practice. But no one was jealous or envious. Those people — Lin, McCarthy, and Santana — were among the best in the business. "It's outside of our bailiwick and I'm acutely aware of the fact we have plenty of work of our own. But Jane is one of our own and we're going to do everything in our power to prevent the culprit who committed this crime from disappearing under the cloak of the coronavirus at a time when law enforcement personnel are stretched and investigatory protocols may have deteriorated."

He studied the faces on the screen. He hoped no one was going to file a complaint about his decision. The reaction he saw was supportive.

He added, "We need to take a moment to realize how fortunate we are as a family. I've heard from a few of you who have family members who are suffering. In a couple of instances, those family members and other close friends have died. And many of you have spouses and significant others who are nurses, doctors and EMTS who are working on the front line. It's creating hardship in families and my heart goes out to all of you.

"But remember something very important. We are all working and being paid. Every two weeks, a paycheck is deposited electronically in your bank account. In fact, you're being paid at a time when your daily expenses have declined."

It was true; there was no need for haircuts, manicures and pedicures, gasoline, dry cleaning, and other incidental expenses.

"As unemployment hovers around 20 percent and as trillions of dollars are being distributed to struggling businesses all over this country, none of us have to worry about how we're going to pay a mortgage or car payment," he continued. "Therefore, I think we're obligated to work harder than ever on behalf of the American people."

That fact was never lost on Katz, who came to government from private practice. As everyone who plied a trade in the courthouse knew, the legal profession ebbed and flowed. Success was measured by what you could do tomorrow. Past success didn't pay the bills for long if an attorney's current performance waned. In the public sector, the pay was constant and the benefits were outstanding, regardless of performance. No one should ever take that for granted, he thought. Plus, it was a good way to bolster morale and build a patriotic sentiment.

"If you were in private practice right now, you'd be sweating it," Katz said. "Clients wouldn't be knocking on your door, partly because they can't go out and commit crimes." Laughs echoed on the conference call. "Let's all give 110 percent this week and every week for the duration of this crisis. Whether you're advising a task force, handling video motions, or checking the status of an investigation, give it your all. Do it for yourself and for your community. Do it for Jane Hutton."

While people initially offered words of consolation and praise for Hutton, the conversation quickly turned into a discussion about how people were coping. Many expressed surprise at the persona their spouses and significant others adopted in the virtual workplace. Others talked about hobbies or projects they had undertaken. People were working on crossword puzzles or building model ships. Some had pulled out old board games gathering dust in attics or basements. Monopoly and Clue were favorites. All of the games were missing pieces and innovation was needed to compensate. Red hotels missing from Monopoly boards were replaced by coins. Miniature chandeliers and other weapons lost in Clue boxes were replaced by thimbles and tiny pieces of jewelry. *It was Mr. Green in the study with the spool of thread.*

Someone on the call started playing music. It was "Lean on Me" by Bill Withers, who had recently died. Someone else played Bob Marley's "No Woman No Cry" and then there was a cascade of songs by Bob Dylan, Kenny Chesney, and the Dixie Chicks. Eventually the conversation began degenerating into water cooler talk and Katz called an end to the video conference.

He then summoned his team to a video chat room at 11:30. Stone had emailed him copies of the reports by the forensics team and he immediately forwarded those reports to the team.

Each of them appeared on his computer screen. McCarthy was encamped in the basement of his home in the center of Old Town near the Torpedo Factory. The walls were filled with posters of iconic pop artists. David and Mai were holding their baby in the kitchen of their two-bedroom apartment in Fairlington Villages in Arlington.

The background showed the door leading to the kitchen and some of the appliances, including the stove. Santana was secluded in the study in Stone's townhome on Prince Street. The background showed a bookcase filled with books, family photos, and the artwork of Stone's nieces and nephews.

"Our entire investigation is going to be conducted online," Katz said. "The internet is the only resource at our disposal. We can't go outside and we can't interact with people. We're confined to our homes, which will serve as our bases of operations. We will employ modern technology to solve the crime. We can employ search engines for research and conduct video conferences on our phones, computers, and tablets.

"We need to consolidate our work, assign responsibilities, avoid duplication, and stay in touch with one another to coordinate efforts as we develop leads. Mac and I discussed the case on the phone yesterday and I'd like him to share his preliminary findings with us. All of you received the reports that were filed by the Alexandria police and you can share what you gleaned from those reports as Mac walks us through his initial thoughts about the crime."

McCarthy leaned into the camera on his computer. His face consumed the screen. "So far, I think we can assume several things," he began. "First, the assailant is probably a woman. I say that because all of the knife wounds were superficial, with one exception, the serious cut to the stomach. My bet is that the assailant did not have significant upper body strength. I know there are women out there who can whip my ass in basketball or baseball. As a general proposition, however, women lack the upper body strength of men and, therefore, I believe it's fair to assume the perpetrator was a woman."

Santana and Lin disagreed. "The superficial cuts could have been caused by a lot of other factors," Santana said. "Height, distance, the use of another instrument. It's a mistake to limit our investigation to one gender or the other."

Lin added, "At this stage, we should be casting a wide net, not a narrow one. Curtis is correct that it could just as easily been a man. In fact, it's conceivable that there were two assailants. So we have to keep an open mind."

McCarthy cleared his throat. "If we're going to make inroads into this case, we have to act quickly," he said. "If, based on the information currently at our disposal, we can make assumptions, we should do so. Trust me, a woman committed this crime."

Katz intervened. "There's value in both approaches. Mac, you have a propensity to immediately hone in on certain likely suspects. It's a methodology that you're comfortable with, and you shouldn't abandon it, even if the others don't adopt it. Please go on."

McCarthy pushed back his chair and stretched with his hands laced behind his head. Then he brushed off his frustration and pushed his face back into the camera. "Second, the assailant and the victim knew one another. Hutton opened the door and welcomed the assailant into her house. There are no signs of forced entry."

He paused for the others to comment. Their silence suggested concurrence. As McCarthy was about to continue, Katz cautioned, "If we conclude that Hutton knew her assailant, we limit the scope of our inquiry as much as we do by assuming the assailant is a woman."

"That's correct," McCarthy said. No one else said anything. It was a basic tenet of police work that assailants knew their victims. Husbands were the most likely suspects when their wives were murdered, and the perpetrator of a garden-variety assault was more likely to live down the street from the victim than in an outlying community. The Department of Justice statistics bore it out. Of course, those statistics were skewed. They didn't take into account the fact that many crimes were never solved. The clearance rate for murder was slightly better than 60 percent, and for aggravated assault it was just over 50 percent. If a criminal played the percentages, there was a 50-50 chance of getting away with a crime. Add to that the effect of COVID-19. It improved the odds that the assailant in

Hutton's case would never be found.

"Okay, then, moving on, I believe the crime was committed as soon as Hutton opened the door, by which I mean the attack occurred in the foyer, not the kitchen, and that it was initiated without any discussion between the parties," McCarthy said.

"How do you figure?" Lin asked. "I'm looking at the reports that Mo emailed us and I don't see that." Katz looked at Lin on the screen. David had departed, taking the baby with him. She was holding copies of the reports, which she had printed out. "There was blood everywhere, on the walls in both the foyer and the kitchen. The stream of blood created by Jane dragging her body across the floor makes it impossible to say where the near fatal stab to the stomach occurred. It looks to me as though it occurred in both rooms. How did you reach that conclusion? Why does it even matter?"

"It means a lot of things," McCarthy replied in a condescending tone. "It rules out heat of passion. This was a deliberate, calculated attempt to kill her. The visitor came with a singular purpose, namely to kill Jane Hutton."

McCarthy's voice grew more passionate as he spoke, reaching a crescendo when he finished. It was like he was advocating his theory of a case in front of a jury. Katz watched as McCarthy's hands flailed in the air. The head of the criminal division was immersed in the case.

Santana said, "The forensic report states there was a large stain of dried blood in the wood floor in the foyer. There was also a pool of blood on the kitchen floor when the police arrived. I can visualize Hutton being stabbed in the foyer, bleeding, falling back, and landing on the tile floor. It's entirely consistent with the evidence. The fact that the front door wasn't closed buttresses this theory. If things progressed normally, Hutton would have closed that door, but she didn't. So she had to be moving backwards right away, probably to avoid being knifed repeatedly.

"However, I don't know if it supports the theory that Hutton and the assailant knew one another. There have been plenty of instances of people opening their doors to complete strangers and being shot immediately, including some pretty infamous cases right here in Alexandria."

Katz interjected a comment. "As we get further into the case, we will find out whether Mac's correct. For now, it helps create a roadmap that we might want to follow as we sort through information. Mac, what else have you got?"

"That's it," he said.

"What about the fact that the assailant never finished the job?" asked Lin.

"What do you think happened?" Katz asked her.

"Sure. I believe something spooked the attacker," she said. "It could have been something inside or outside of the house. I don't know. But something happened. Otherwise, the attacker would have finished the job and Hutton would be dead. And that leads me to another observation. I don't know whether the attacker was a man or a woman and I'm not sure whether it matters if the attack commenced in the foyer or the kitchen. But I think it's noteworthy that the assailant was an amateur. The job was never finished. This wasn't a professional hit. No one put out a contract on Jane Hutton. We aren't looking for a conspiracy and we aren't even looking for someone with a criminal record. We're looking for a regular person, just like one of us, except someone who was motivated to kill her. That person got flustered, left a door open, and allowed her to survive."

Katz studied each member of the team as they spoke. It was like viewing them through the window of an interview room. For all of the meetings they held around the conference table in his office, this was a unique experience. He was able to observe Lin's quiet resolve, Santana's seemingly detached aloofness, and McCarthy's passionate intensity.

"I agree with you," McCarthy said. "We aren't looking for someone who has a criminal history or who was paid to kill her.

We're looking for a close friend or family member, probably a woman. And it's someone in plain view who we would least suspect of a crime like this."

The front doorbell rang.
Hutton quickly thought who it might be. It could be that neighbor, the nosy one. It could be her mother, who promised to drop by but had not yet made an appearance. Or it could be him, returning. Whoever it was, they should have notified her that they were coming over. She looked through the peep hole. She was not surprised. "I had a premonition you might drop by," she said, opening the door.
Two fast steps inside. "You never should have started this," said the visitor. "You've left me no other choice." The door swung back, but Hutton did not have a chance to close it. She was already moving away from the visitor, sensing danger. The visitor moved forward, expressing more words of anger and betrayal. Then a push. A sharp pain. She looked down.
"What have you done?" She was in disbelief. "Are you mad? Are you totally out of your mind?" She clutched the door frame with a hand dripping with blood. She fell to the kitchen floor. In a weak and desperate voice, she whispered to the electronic assistant on the kitchen counter, "Get help. Call 911."
"The emergency medical team has been alerted," the device responded. "Their arrival time is less than five minutes."
The attacker stopped and stared at the device. "Cancel that call!" No response. The assailant unplugged the device from the wall socket and left with it by the patio door. An instant later, the assailant wondered whether the front door had ever closed. It didn't matter. She was dead or close to it. No way would she be able to call for help. And it was too dangerous for the assailant to go back to check if the door was shut. Plus, if she wasn't dead, she deserved to suffer. Dying fast was too easy. Prolonging the suffering was much more satisfying.

"Can I have your attention?" Katz said. "Some of you look like you're fading out."

"Just thinking," McCarthy replied.

"I think we're all dreaming up scenarios," Lin said. "There are so many permutations dancing around in my mind right now. I mean, I'm thinking that maybe this was a hate crime. Maybe the assailant wanted Jane to die slowly."

Katz understood that they all had theories in their heads. The best police investigators and trial attorneys — both prosecutors and defense attorneys — often delved into the heart of a case without knowing the identity of the perpetrator or what really happened, if they ever knew. There were too many variables to a case. The best in the business spun tales in their heads. After all, clients lied, witnesses had difficulty recollecting, and evidence was often misleading. The *truth* was what you made it. The system had mischief built into it. The standard for truth in a court of law was not beyond all doubt. The standard was *beyond a reasonable doubt*. A good defense attorney could persuade a jury to acquit a guilty man under that standard and a bad prosecutor could get an innocent man convicted. The men and women who managed court cases sometimes convinced others, and sometimes themselves, of the *truth* of lies and falsehoods.

Katz said, "Let's each focus in one area. We can share our findings daily. Mai, I'd like you to focus on Jane's old law firm, particularly her former clients and opposing counsel in contentious litigation. Were there any cases that created a poisonous atmosphere? If so, who were the people with whom she had toxic relations?

"Curtis, you look at the cases she handled in our office and the people she interacted with here, including clerks and judges. Was she getting involved in any cases that were particularly controversial and could have caused someone to strike out against her?

"And Mac, I want you to look into her close friends and neighbors, including members of any clubs she belonged to and activities in which she was engaged. Did she have enemies? If so, did anyone ever threaten her? Were there any past instances of violence of any sort?"

"Including significant others?" McCarthy asked.

"Of course," Katz replied. "According to your theory, the assailant was someone close to her. That includes lovers and significant others. Any other questions?" There were none. "Remember," he said, "everyone is a suspect, no one is excluded, and everyone is capable of doing something terrible given the right set of circumstances."

"I have a question," Lin said. "The people in her firm are not going to be able to talk about cases with me. I'm going to run into confidentiality problems."

"Not necessarily," Katz said. "Begin with a general inquiry. I'd start with her executive assistant or some attorney who served as her confidant. One good contact will give you a feel as to whether she was in any poisonous relationships at the firm, either professional or personal. You should be able to do that without broaching confidentiality."

"What about me?" asked Reese, appearing on the screen behind Lin. He held the sleeping baby against his chest. His dark hair was ruffled; he wore a dark blue T-shirt. "What's my assignment?"

"You work with Detective Stone," Katz said. "She's leading the police investigation. I don't know whether her people are computer savvy or how much bandwidth current exists at the department. We'll run every lead through her, and you can be our liaison."

The call ended and everyone got to work. Lin had converted the loft in their apartment into an office, replete with a stand-up desk composed of plastic crates. Her commute to work was a trip up a spiral staircase. Once settled, she needed only two emails to locate Hutton's former administrative assistant at Stephens Babcock & Brazier. His name was Blair Craig. When he appeared online, he was hard to see because there was a window behind him and his face was in shadow.

Ironically, Hutton's assault occurred at a time when all major crime was down. Normally an attack at home on Easter Sunday would be front page stuff. But it was buried in the metro news as people focused on an existential threat. The number of people dying of the virus rose each day. Everyone's primary concern was the health and safety of their family and themselves.

Craig choked up when he started to talk. Jane Hutton was a mentor. He found it incomprehensible that anyone would injure her. He asked whether it was possible that it was a case of mistaken identity. "Have you seen picture of her mother?" Craig asked. "They look identical, down to the last detail. The attacker might have gotten the wrong woman."

His question had not been discussed previously with Katz. Lin thought it was fascinating to speculate that the attack might be a mistake. The team was focused upon friends, enemies, and court cases involving Hutton. But what if the inquiry was completely misdirected? If the intended victim was Tricia Barton, then they were completely off the track.

"Strange things happen in cases," Craig said. "Sometimes the person who's leading the investigation is the one responsible for the crime. And sometimes the victim is just an innocent party in the wrong place at the wrong time. Investigations can get entirely sidetracked."

Lin asked, "Are you an attorney?"

He laughed. "No, but with a name like Blair Craig, everyone thinks I am. Isn't everyone with two first names a lawyer? I don't even have a college degree, just an associate's degree from NOVA," referring to the Northern Virginia Community College. "What about you?"

She explained she had a bachelor's degree in clinical psychology from Marymount University and planned to attend law school once her husband earned his degree and passed the bar. "But I'm reassessing things now," she added. "We've started a family and I'm not sure the time is right for me to go back to school. Maybe in a few years. This whole COVID-19 thing is freaking me out. It's making me question what I want to do with my life. I thought it was the law, but now I'm not so sure. All I really want to do is take care of our son, to try to make the world a better place. I'm actually thinking of turning to medicine."

They hit it off, two young millennials trying to figure out what to do with their lives while caught in the spiral of COVID-19.

"Has this whole coronavirus thing affected your thinking?" she asked him.

"No, not really," Craig replied. "I mean, I don't have a family. I don't even have a serious girlfriend or anything. I don't think about making the world a better place for the next generation. I do think a lot about making the planet better, though. You know, cleaner air and stuff like that. Fewer guns. Stuff like that.

"I don't even know if I even really believe this coronavirus thing. It's like mostly old people, so maybe it's nature culling the herd. I'll bet more young people die of drug overdoses and suicide than from this thing, and nobody ever suggested closing down businesses because there's a drug epidemic in this country and teens are taking their own lives because they're alienated and don't see any reason to live. No one gives a damn about things like that, you know."

"I agree with you, to a point," said Lin. "I don't think drugs and teen suicide get nearly as much attention as they should. They just write them off as statistics. But this coronavirus is real. There's no vaccine. It's a worldwide pandemic. If we weren't doing the social distancing, a lot more people would be dying. I'll be honest." She lowered her voice. "It scares the shit out of me."

"I consider it an annoyance more than anything else," he said. "With this six feet of separation, I'm pretty much stuck in my apartment near Chinatown, which sucks. I can't meet my friends at bars and my dating is confined to online stuff."

"How's that going?" Lin giggled. "I can at least hug my baby and my husband. I think I'd go out of my mind if I couldn't hold them. I need that human contact, you know? Online dating has such…limitations."

"Actually, it's not that bad," he laughed. "I've met a girl and we go out once a week. Between dates, we either read the same book or visit some place online so we have a shared point of reference. I'm actually enjoying it."

"Really?"

"You sound surprised or like you don't believe me."

"A little of both, to be honest."

"Well, it's true. I guess it's platonic, you know. But it works for me."

As they talked, Lin tried to study his gestures and expressions. "How come you've got your camera positioned toward the window?" she asked. "It hides your face. Do you do that on purpose? Can you move so I can see you better?"

"No problem." He moved to the other side of the room, so that he was facing the light from the window. He turned on the overhead light. His eyes were sunken in his face. He stared vacantly at her.

"A birth defect," he said. "I'm legally blind. I still managed to graduate from high school and earn an associate degree, like I told you. I'm proud of what I've accomplished. I've never subscribed to the notion that I have a disability and Jane never treated me as though I have one."

Lin bowed her head. "Very impressive, Blair," she said.

"What's that I hear in the background?"

"That's my son. He's downstairs with my husband. I'm up in a loft. We avoid bringing him up here. He's six months old. There's a railing and all, but I think he could get stuck in it, and I don't want to risk him getting stuck or falling."

"What's his name?"

"His name is Min-Jun. It means handsome, sharp, quick, clever, and talented. We honored my Korean heritage," she explained. We also call him Mike."

"Be like Mike," Craig said. "Great program, *The Last Dance*. Are you watching it on ESPN?"

Lin just laughed.

"How are you doing in terms of getting formula and all that stuff?" Craig asked. "I read this morning in *The Washington Post*'s 'Coronavirus Digest' that parents are having difficulty getting baby formula."

"I saw that too," she said. "Fortunately, we've been lucky finding formula and diapers. There's a co-op here and parents have been really good about sharing everything. We haven't been back to the pediatrician yet, but hopefully they've got things under control. Thanks for asking."

"No problem," Craig said. "So back to Jane Hutton. What can I do for you?"

"I'm interested in figuring out her footprint at Stephens Babcock and whether there were any particularly tumultuous clients or cases that should be considered as part of the investigation."

"I'll bet you're expecting me to say I can't say anything because of client confidentiality and refer you to one of the senior partners."

Lin laughed. "Exactly. That's what I discussed with Mo about an hour ago."

"Mo Katz?"

"The one and only."

"So when you see your boss, tell him that Blair Craig said hello." Lin saw a smile spread across his face. "I lived in Alexandria when I was in high school. I got into trouble when I was a kid. I was pissed because of my disability." He pointed at his eyes. "I blamed everyone for it. I blamed God. I blamed my parents. So I went around vandalizing stuff. Cars, houses. You name it. He was a city prosecutor in those days. Long story short, Mo Katz cut me some slack. Actually, he cut me a lot of slack. He seemed to understand what I was going through. He related to me.

"He never made excuses for me and he forced me to complete some pretty intense counseling. But because of him, I avoided getting a felony conviction on my record. I was already over 18 at the time, so it would have been on my record forever. I didn't realize it at the time, but he did me a huge favor. So next time you talk to him say I said hello and thank you."

While Craig was talking, Reese joined Lin upstairs. He caught her eye, smiled, folded his hands as in prayer, tipped his head, and placed his hands beside his check. Mike was asleep. She smiled back. "It's nice to hear you say that, Blair. This is my husband, David," she said, waving him closer. "We met Mr. Katz in 2017 and helped him with a case on Daingerfield Island by the airport. He basically adopted us after that. Whether he was a prosecutor or a defense attorney, he's always found a way to help people."

"True that," Craig said. "Now back to Jane Hutton. You're not going to have any pushback about confidentiality from me. It's actually pretty simple. She was totally consumed with one client, namely the BOM." He was referring to the Bank of Magellan.

"I worked on that case," Lin said excitedly.

He laughed. "I think we might have met. Were you at that conference in the U.S. Attorney's office where Jane basically shredded Mac McCarthy during a settlement conference?"

"Yes, except I wouldn't say she shredded Mac. He was stalling for time. He has an uncanny ability to make you believe one thing while he's doing the opposite. He was just playing dumb. He was actually two steps ahead of her. Anyway, that's neither here nor there. I do remember one of her staff wearing sunglasses and thinking that it was a little odd."

"That was me," he said. "Six degrees of separation, I suppose. I don't remember you being in the room."

"So what can you tell me about BOM?" she asked.

"They were scumbags," Craig said. "The whole lot of them. They laundered the money used to buy those IEDs that killed American soldiers. They were never sorry for what they did. She detested them for it. She used to tell me all the time that they made her sick.

"She finagled the company into pleading to both civil and criminal charges. They didn't want to do it at first. They were pissed that Mr. Katz raised the stakes by threatening a criminal prosecution. She told them they would lose in the courtroom and in the court of public opinion. They didn't care. She went around the board's back straight to the CEO of the company and persuaded him to cave. The board never forgave her for what happened. We lost BOM as a client as a result of that fiasco. If Mr. Katz hadn't hired her, Jane would have gotten the boot from Stephens Babcock. The relationship was that bad."

"Really?"

"Yeah. There's a whole backstory. It never made headlines and most people don't know about it. I think Katz knew that. I always thought he offered her a job in his office because she'd forced the settlement. I mean, when you think about it, she wasn't qualified to head the civil division in the U.S. Attorney's office. Plus, from what I knew about the case, it was never a slam dunk that the prosecution was going to prevail if the case went to trial. I think he knew she'd done him a favor and put herself in jeopardy by doing it. He threw her a lifeline."

Lin looked at Reese. It had never crossed their minds. Katz was a sphinx. He was always playing a game of three-dimensional chess. It was entirely possible that he offered Hutton a job last year as a reward for helping him with a case, they thought. It would also explain why Katz wanted to find her attacker. He felt personally responsible.

"Do you think the board's dislike for her would have led them to attack her as a vendetta?" Lin asked.

"It's the first thing I thought of when I heard someone had tried to kill her," Craig said. "I once went to dinner with some BOM board members and I felt I had to take a shower by the time I got home. Everything about them — the way they looked, talked, dressed, smelled — made me think of gangsters and mafia.

"Hell, I would have dumped them as a client. She didn't because she wanted the challenge. But to your question: Do I think there might have been a vendetta of some sort? Yes. The chair of BOM is Suzanne Marconi. She's a bitch. I wouldn't put anything past her."

As he spoke, Lin searched BOM. "The company is based in Chicago, right?" she asked. "Is that where Ms. Marconi is located?"

"No. First, BOM moved its corporate headquarters to New York at the first of the year. And Marconi maintains her office in Washington, where the government affairs office is located. She's not an employee of BOM, just serves on the board. She actually operates a slew of minority women-owned businesses in D.C. and subcontracts with larger defense contractors throughout the country. She's also a lobbyist for a lot of big name people. And I mean big, as in companies the size of Microsoft and Oracle. GlassGrass, for example. BOM is just one way she expanded her profile. The corporate office is pretty swanky, although I'm sure it's deserted these days. She's probably holed up at her mansion on Foxhall Road."

Lin thanked Craig and promised to give his regards to Katz. She also suggested they get together once the coronavirus passed and people could shorten their social distance. He said he'd like to do that. After she ended the conversation, Lin went online and looked up Suzanne Marconi. Her photo showed a fit, professional-looking woman, around 60, with short white hair and penetrating blue eyes.

*

HUTTON'S ASSAILANT was now acutely aware that the U.S. Attorney's office was investigating the case. The assailant had not anticipated this development. In fact, the exact opposite was expected, namely that the investigation would languish because of the coronavirus. It was sensible to believe resources would be stretched, lab analysis delayed, crucial personnel unavailable, and standard operating procedures discarded.

The assailant knew that the crime itself — killing someone who answered the front door — would be difficult to solve even without a pandemic raging through the community. It was the kind of crime that was difficult to solve because it was so simple. Simplicity was beguiling. *"Knock. Talk. Enter. Kill. Exit. Murder."* That was the game plan. Those were the words composed by the man convicted of the Dunning murder. And how long had it taken to arrest someone for that crime? Over a decade! And the arrest was only made following two similar murders that provided the Alexandria police with additional clues.

The assailant was a bit of a criminologist. The assailant knew what it took to sustain a conviction and to win an acquittal. Clues had been left behind at the crime scene to lead investigators in the wrong direction. Would those clues mislead the U.S. attorney and his team?

Katz's involvement was not the only surprise. The bigger problem was that Jane Hutton was alive. How did that happen? It seemed a foregone conclusion that she would die. She was lying on the kitchen floor immobilized in a pool of blood caused by a hole in her stomach. It was like a victim of the coronavirus being hooked up to a ventilator and surviving! The odds of that happening were 50-50. Those odds were a lot better than the odds assigned to Hutton when she was left for dead on the tile floor.

Did it make sense to go to Baltimore and finish the job? Or did it make more sense to run?

The assailant tried not to panic. There were a lot of clues to mislead, confuse and confound the investigators. Even if everything failed and the assailant was likely to be arrested, there was a game plan to minimize a conviction and guarantee a lenient sentence.

As for running, where would the assailant go? States were imposing travel restrictions. Neighboring states like Maryland, Delaware, and the Carolinas had stringent restrictions. North Carolina police were checking the residency of drivers trying to get over to the Outer Banks. Taking a train was almost out of the question. Imagine arriving at Grand Central Station today? Finally, airlines had cancelled most international flights and few domestic flights were operating. Even if one could fly out of BWI Marshall, Reagan National, or Dulles International, where could one go? Most hotels and motels were closed. Home rentals were hard to find. Nearly all travel by road, rail, or air was untenable.

The most sensible option was to disrupt the investigation and prepare to minimize the damage if the crime was solved and a court case appeared on the horizon.

*

STONE WORKED in her corner office on the second floor at police headquarters. She opened a mapping app on her computer and surveyed the area around Slaters Lane. She studied it from an overhead angle as though she was commanding a drone. Then she dropped down and virtually walked the neighborhood streets familiarizing herself with every nook and cranny.

Slaters Lane extended from the Mount Vernon Trail adjacent the Potomac River to Route 1. The neighborhoods around Slaters Lane were a mix of new and established townhomes, apartments, restaurants, and commercial dwellings. Stone went around Hutton's home and then went back to an aerial view of the street. She repeated her survey twice as though she was a street cop looking for clues on the ground.

The forensic folks had found a bloody print of a heel in the kitchen and a matching footprint in a muddy area near the patio. Any additional outside footprints were washed out by Sunday night's storm. The single heel print inside the house was found on the kitchen tile. There was a small smudge of blood on the kitchen counter which Stone concluded was caused when the assailant grabbed a paper towel to wipe the blood off the heel of his or her footwear.

The wavy pattern from the heel was easily identified as that of a popular woman's duck shoe. It was size 6. The footprint on the mud matched the make and size of the heel mark in the kitchen.

Stone decided to keep the information close hold, which meant not sharing it with Katz and his team. Katz volunteered to help her, not the other way around, she reasoned. She was under no obligation to keep him fully informed. Her instincts told her to withhold the information. She had no intention of telling Santana about it. She decided preliminarily not to share the information with Reese. Then she reversed her decision and called him.

"Listen," she said, "I'm going to share some information with you. You're part of my team at the police department. You don't work for Mo Katz. As such, you are not to share the information with the federal prosecution, including Mai. Are you okay with that?"

Reese hesitated. He never withheld anything from Mai. She was his partner. "I don't know," he said. "Why?"

"I have my reasons. It's the way I want it. Maybe I'm not a team player. If you can abide my request, I'll share the information, which is my preference. But if you're uncomfortable, I'll keep it to myself. No big deal."

"Are you going to tell Curtis?"

"Okay, David, thank you. Goodbye." She hung up the phone. *Am I going to tell Curtis?* she repeated to herself. *How stupid is that boy?*

The phone rang. It was Reese calling back. "Yeah," she said. She listened. "Okay. Just don't get your panties all in a bunch. This is no big deal. It's just that what happens in my world stays in my world. I'm cutting you in because you're part of my team. Don't disappoint me." Then she told him about the footprint and she shared her suspicions.

"Geez," Reese said when she finished. "Thanks for trusting me, Sherry. I won't let you down."

"I know you won't," she said. "Otherwise I would have followed my initial instinct and kept you out. Now I want you to do something."

"Whatever you want."

"I want you to be my foot soldier. There are a lot of commercial businesses and restaurants in that area. Were any of the businesses open Sunday, particularly the restaurants filling carry-out orders? How about people who live near Hutton's place? Do any of them have front door camera systems? If so, ask them to share their footage from 3 p.m. on the 12th. Was anyone outside flying a drone of any sort? Or taking pictures? In other words, canvass the area for any electronics or equipment that could have picked up the action around Hutton's house. There's got to be something."

"How do you want me to do that? Do you want me to actually go down to Slaters Lane and start knocking on doors?"

"No, silly. I want you to do it all remotely and virtually. I don't want you to take a step outside of your home. You should be able to find everyone you need online."

"Got it," he said. "And thanks again for trusting me."

Stone wasn't sure he would keep her confidence. She sensed Reese was insecure. If she had to put odds on it, she would wager that he would eventually break. But that was okay. Stone knew the only person in whom he would confide was Lin, and Lin was smart enough and strong enough to hold her secret.

"Oh, I have one more question?"

"What is it, David?"

"Forgive me for asking, but do you share everything you do in your professional life with Curtis? I'm just wondering."

She smiled. "David, I don't share everything I do in my *personal* life with Curtis. Does that answer your question?"

*

SANTANA OBTAINED access to the database of all of the civil cases handled by the U.S. Attorney's office. The first case he looked up was the BOM settlement. It was only a reference point. Hutton joined the office after that plea went down. She was counsel for the defendant.

The file revealed that Hutton opened a series of inquiries into various aspects of BOM's operations. Santana wondered whether Hutton had taken her confidential and privileged information with her and was now using it against the company. He sensed the irony. She had spent years of her life fighting to keep BOM out of trouble; maybe she was now on the verge of exposing its wrongdoing.

He wondered if it signified a pattern. Had she taken additional information about other clients and cases from her old firm? He looked at all of the civil inquiries that she had initiated in the past six months.

There were two cases that caught his attention, both involving a New Jersey company that handled massive federal contracts with the U.S. Department of Housing and Community Development. The company provided comprehensive cleaning services to federal buildings. One of the cases was new. It proposed augmenting existing cleaning services to cover offices, elevators, stairwells, hallways, and conference rooms to protect workers against the coronavirus. The services would commence in April while the buildings stood mostly vacant, and the services would continue for two years, based upon an assumption that recovery from COVID-19 would be a "swoosh" rather than a V-shaped recovery.

Santana discovered that the company had previously been represented by Stephens Babcock & Brasier in cases alleging price fixing, fraud, and contract violations. The firm successfully defended the company in all of those cases. Hutton was not involved in the litigation, but she was at the firm when the litigation took place and the attorneys who handled the cases reported to her. Santana reasoned that, as in the case of BOM, Hutton knew of malfeasance committed by the company that was neither exposed nor remedied in court due to the superior legal services of her firm.

Santana worked in a gabled attic room in Stone's home that had a narrow window overlooking Prince Street. The one-way street was a central artery for traffic headed to Washington Street and the waterfront. Normally cars, trucks, and buses went down the street throughout the day. Now the street was deserted. The silence was eerie.

Occasionally, one or two people walked by, usually with a pet or a baby carriage. As a person approached in the opposite direction, the parties would move away from one another, some walking into the empty street. Several of the individuals were wearing masks. People seemed afraid to get within 20 feet of one another, let alone 6 feet. It was as though they feared the coronavirus would leap off another person's shoulder and land on them. Maybe that was a good thing, he thought, but it seemed a little excessive. He questioned whether things would get back to normal or if the uncertainty and mistrust would linger for months to come.

"Find anything?" Stone asked. Santana turned around.

"I thought you were at work."

"I was, but I came home to get something to eat," she said. "Nothing's open out there except for carryout and I forgot to place an order, so I thought I'd come home to eat."

"Can't you just go there and place an order?"

"I suppose, but then I'd have to stand outside. And they want to do the transactions over the phone before you arrive. So it's almost more hassle than it's worth. Why, am I disturbing you?" She glanced out the window. "It's so strange," she said. "I used to complain about the noise from the traffic. Now I find myself missing it."

It occurred to Santana that she had never dropped by the house unannounced in the three years they'd been dating. Before the lockdown they rarely if ever ate together in the house. It was always at some restaurant on King or Washington Street. The coronavirus was disrupting patterns of behavior. In this instance, it was a good one. "How about finishing that lentil dish we had last night?" he asked, getting up from the oak desk positioned under the window.

"Sounds good." Leaning over the desk to peer at his computer array, she asked, "So, did you find anything?"

"Only that Hutton was a crusader," he said. "She was looking at cases involving some of her old clients. I think she wanted to prosecute them for things they'd gotten away with in the past."

Stone furrowed her brow. "What are you talking about?" she asked. "She couldn't do that. It would violate confidentiality. She'd get disbarred." She slid into his seat and studied the three monitors open on the desk. "It's something else," she muttered. "And probably something sinister or illegal."

Santana left her alone. He went downstairs, took three plastic containers out of the refrigerator and placed them in the microwave. Then he cut a few pieces of the beer bread that he'd made over the weekend. He mixed the contents of the containers together and dished them out onto two plates.

He opened a fresh bottle of Malbec. He studied the label. *Wine of San Juan – Argentina. 2019.* Ah, he thought to himself. Pre-COVID-19. Nothing to worry about. He wondered how people would greet wine with a 2020 vintage. 2020: The Year of the Coronavirus. Would the grapes be suspect? Would people be afraid to handle the bottles? As he studied the label, he noticed a sticker that recommended downloading an app to learn more about the wine. He expected to see "Safe to Drink" or "Take Your Wine into Your Own Hands, Not Your Life" on bottles with a 2020 vintage. Perhaps the grapes would be subject to special cleanings. Maybe the vineyard would use Clorox.

While Santana mused over the wine, Stone studied the cases open on Santana's computer. She ran comparative analyses, took some notes, drew circles around some names and boxes around others, connected lines between the circles and the boxes, and wrote down her conclusions at the bottom of a sheet of paper.

Dinner was cold by the time she came down from the attic room. Santana had not eaten but he had consumed most of the wine. She inspected the bottle and smiled. He offered her a stemmed glass and they clinked, the lead crystal making a melodic ring.

"Perspective is an amazing thing," she said. "Two people can look at the same thing and see two entirely different realities. I understand your bias. Mo hired Jane and you've worked with her in the office. She's fighting for her life and you're trying to identify her attacker. So I'm going to cut you a little slack as I criticize your powers of deduction." He swirled the wine in his glass and gazed at her. "You're a brilliant investigator and I love you, baby, but you blew it in your evaluation of this case," she said.

She lay down the paper with her notes, drawings, and conclusions. "Jane Hutton isn't a caped crusader, Curtis. Look over this paper and then go back upstairs and reexamine those files. Hutton was not going to open up any investigations. I think she might have been laying the groundwork to blackmail someone by exposing their past misconduct."

She sat down and started eating.

"It's better hot," he said.

She shook her head. "This is fine," she said with her mouth full of food. She grabbed some of the beer bread and dipped it into her bowl. "Check out my diagrams and see if my conclusions add up," she said. She glanced up at him from her food. He looked dejected. "It really doesn't matter which of us is right," she said. "You see a white knight and I see a black witch. Either way, there might be individuals out there who were interested in silencing Hutton. We're both after the same thing. We're just seeing it from a different point of view."

Santana was speechless. He always pegged Hutton as one of the forces for good; a white knight, to use Stone's terminology. It never crossed his mind that she might be gaming the system. Stone's allegation was a serious one, namely that Hutton was using her position for personal gain.

"This is delicious," Stone said. "It's amazing how many dishes are better the second night after you make them. I think the sauce got a little thicker or something. You are a phenomenal cook." She looked at him. "Anyway, I might be wrong about what I think I'm seeing. One thing I'm not wrong about is your cooking."

While she ate, Santana inspected her analysis. She was right: Two people could look at the same item and see different things. He saw holes in her analysis. Maybe she was envious of Jane Hutton, he thought, and wanted to knock her down. Maybe it was something else. But he was done thinking for the day. He emptied the remainder of the bottle equally in the two glasses. The puzzle was still going to be with them tomorrow.

"Let me go back and look this over some more," he said.

"Hmm," she said, raising a hand with a spoon. She swallowed the food in her mouth. "Not so fast, big boy. I'm home for the afternoon. Let's make the most of it. It'll be sort of novel doing it midday, don't you think?" She raised her eyebrows. "Might even border on decadent. The work can wait. Our assailant isn't going anywhere. He's holed up for the duration."

"Oh, I wasn't planning on going back to work now," Santana said, staring at her intently. "But Mac said it's probably a woman," he added.

"No, honey," she said, finishing her food. "It was a man. And a devilish man at that."

Chapter Three: BARTON

IT WAS a cool autumn evening in mid-October 2019. The Principle Gallery in Alexandria was packed. The normally sedate art gallery had been transformed into a reception hall to welcome Jane Hutton to the U.S. Attorney's office as the new deputy for civil litigation. People stood shoulder to shoulder in the art gallery a block from the Potomac River and the Torpedo Factory. There were handshakes, kisses on both cheeks, pats on the back, and whispers in ears throughout the room. There were close-up selfies with people squished together. Everyone was in a festive mood.

It was considered a coup for Katz to have persuaded Hutton to leave a prestigious silk-stocking firm. While people might have understood her taking a job as the head of the civil branch at Justice or as counsel to the president, they were flabbergasted to hear she settled for a position in EDVA, the Eastern District of Virginia, which covered Northern Virginia, Richmond, and Norfolk. The only logical explanation was that she wanted to work alongside Mo Katz, a legend in his own right.

"Jane," said a woman coming up behind a statuesque figure with striking red hair. The redhead turned. "Oh, I'm sorry," the woman said. "I thought you were the guest of honor." The red-haired woman said no apology was needed. She was Hutton's mother, Tricia Barton. It was flattering to be mistaken as her daughter. "Oh, Ms. Barton," said the guest. "It's an equal honor to meet you. Jane speaks very highly of you. People say she took this job to learn from the master, Mo Katz, but I think she took it to move into the public sector and emulate you."

Barton smiled. When the guest had said, "Jane speaks very highly of you," Barton was tempted to reply, "If she speaks about me at all," but that would have been petty and only feed further rumors. So she refrained. Instead, she said, "My daughter has no need to try to emulate me." But she couldn't resist adding a zinger. "After all, she'll never come close to matching my accomplishments, so why bother." Barton smiled. The guest looked shocked. "I'm joking," she said quickly. "My daughter is a superstar. I expect her to succeed Mr. Katz within a year and get elected to the U.S. Senate in a couple of years. Who's up for election in 2022? Neither Warner nor Kaine would stand a chance if she faced off against them."

Now the guest laughed heartily, as did others circling Hutton's mother, though everyone's laughter was tingled with nervousness. The comment might have been made tongue-in-cheek, the guest thought to herself, but one could never be entirely sure of it. Tricia Barton was an enigma. In her prime, she was a force of nature. There were few women who exceeded her in prominence in the 1980s. She had briefly been considered a possible running mate for Walter Mondale before Geraldine Ferraro was selected to join the presidential ticket against Ronald Reagan. Those were lofty years of firsts for women: Sandra Day O'Connor appointed to the Supreme Court, Sally Ride roaring into space aboard *Challenger*, and Elizabeth Dole named secretary of the Department of Transportation.

Barton was right up there with them, being compared to Pamela Harriman in some quarters for her salon. She was a high-powered attorney, shifting back and forth from the private to the public sector in both Democratic and Republican administrations, serving as a senior partner in a philanthropy, and a confidant of senators and Supreme Court justices. Her opinions were sought and shared frequently, including during an occasional appearance on "The McLaughlin Group." She was on the cover of *Time*, *Life*, and *The Washingtonian*. It was a while ago, but, to people of a certain age, she was an icon, and to everyone else she was still a formidable presence.

"Mother." Barton turned. "I'd like to introduce you to Mo Katz." Hutton was standing beside the U.S. attorney. Barton looked at Katz and said, "*Fatta la legge, trovato l'inganno.*" It was his signature line in private practice, the one he used repeatedly in opening statement in nearly every jurisdiction in the metropolitan area. Loosely translated it meant "Every law has its loophole." No one employed that principle better than Mo Katz. It enabled him to win acquittals for white-collar criminals and petit misdemeanants. "I'm a fan, Mo," she said, "and it's nice to finally meet you. I hope you're closing those loopholes now that you're on the right side of the law."

"I'm trying," Katz said. He marveled at how much she resembled her daughter. In fact, they practically looked like sisters. He decided to avoid any comparisons — he was sure such comments had been made all the time — and said in a self-deprecating tone, "No one better than a fox to guard the henhouse."

Mac McCarthy swept in between mother and daughter. "I don't recall so many people of such notoriety in one place since Sherry Stone was honored for valor at the Lyceum last year," he said. It was true. Members of Congress, judges, local politicians, the captains of commerce, media personalities, and prominent attorneys had turned out for that event. "It's hard to tell the two of you apart," he said, putting one arm around Hutton and the other around Barton. "Actually, to be honest, Jane, you look like the older sister."

Barton loved it. "The older sister," she repeated. Then she squeezed McCarthy's arm. "I'll keep this one," she said.

A jazz ensemble played in the background. Snowe wedged her way into the group. Katz introduced her to Barton. Waiters came with trays filled with shrimp and salmon, cheese and olives, and champagne and wine. Everyone feasted, talked, and danced. "So that's Jane Hutton's mother," Snowe said when she and Katz moved to the dance floor. "It's uncanny how much they resemble one another. People have told me that they have some kind of strange symbiotic relationship. They do everything exactly like one another. They dress the same. They act the same. They apparently both live in the same model of house near Slaters Lane and both houses are designed exactly the same, inside and out. Same furnishings, appliances, you name it. Weird, huh?"

Part Two

The Runaround
Thursday, April 16, to Sunday, April 19

Lights out tonight, trouble in the heartland
Got a head-on collision, smashin' in my guts man
I'm caught in a crossfire that I don't understand…

– *Badlands* by Bruce Springsteen

Chapter One: JUDKIS

THE CITY, state, nation, and world remained in shutdown mode. The number of people with COVID-19 continued to rise. There were now 1.9 million cases world-wide with 127,601 deaths. In the U.S., 609,685 cases had been identified and 26,059 people had died. Those sobering numbers did not diminish or deter the team from doing its work. The key for each of them was to remain healthy and ensure the health and safety of their homes.

For Lin, it included the wellbeing of her husband and son. She decided to proceed to vaccinations, knowing that some of her friends were postponing visits to the pediatrician. From everything Lin read, the virus was forgiving to the young. She figured it was safe to get the immunizations and that delaying was irresponsible.

For his part, Santana tried to make sure he didn't risk contracting the virus and passing it along to Stone. He did the grocery shopping and the trips to the local pharmacy, wearing protective masks and latex gloves every time he went outside. Haircuts and dry cleaning were no longer on the weekly schedule, and he had not filled their SUV with gas in two months. He was concerned that Stone continued to go into the office each day, but he understood that her dedication to law enforcement was like that of the nurses and doctors who returned to hospitals each day to tend to the sick. He admired and respected her dedication, along with everyone else who put duty to others ahead of their personal wellbeing. If nurses did not walk the ward and grocers did not stock aisles with food, they would all succumb to the effects of the virus.

McCarthy was making the most of his confinement. He had built a makeshift gym, office, library, and deli in his apartment in Old Town near the Torpedo Factory. He watched and read everything. He had seen some anniversary photos of the ill-fated April flight of Apollo 13 flight and likened his apartment to something like the Odyssey space capsule and the Aquarius lunar landing module. He moved from one cold room to the other and occasionally looked out his window at a world standing still. He could not remember an April as cold or as wet as this year.

As part of the Hutton investigation, McCarthy contacted the local homeowners association to which she belonged, a loose federation of property owners in North Alexandria who lived in the vicinity of Slaters Lane.

McCarthy sent emails to the SNL Board members. SNL stood for Slaters & Neighborhood Lanes Homeowners Association. People took great pride in the name and reveled in the confusion with the popular "Saturday Night Live" TV show. It reminded him that he needed to check out the videos of the latest SNL show that was recorded remotely without anyone in the studio.

The first person to respond to his inquiry was Hutton's next-door neighbor, Kyle Judkis, who contacted him within an hour. As soon as he received the response, McCarthy searched online for information about her. He searched social media sites, Alexandria tax records, and links that appeared on the search engine. In a matter of minutes, he learned that she was single, 38, employed by the National Institutes of Health, graduated cum laude from Boston University, and enjoyed cycling and hiking.

He suggested they do a Skype call and within minutes her image appeared on a box on his computer screen. She wore thick black-rimmed glasses; had a long, thin face; and her hair was matted down. She wore a Nationals' T-shirt, red with a white curly W.

"No Opening Day," he said.

"No World Series banner raised either," she replied. "The way things are going, they'll be the first team to hold the championship for two years based on a single win."

"That's pretty good," he replied, "but I hope you're wrong. They're already playing baseball in Japan with pictures of people seated in empty ballparks. I hear they're trying to reconfigure the leagues and play games in Florida, maybe in empty stadiums. Just so long as they're broadcast on television, I'm okay with it."

Having established a personal connection with the interviewee, McCarthy asked her about Hutton.

"She kept to herself," Judkis said. "We didn't interact much. That's pretty much par for the course around here. Everyone does their own thing. No one really pays attention to anyone else's business. We're all too busy for that. At least I am, always on the go, you know." Without further prodding, she added, "I only saw her in the morning. And in the evening. She gets a newspaper delivered. Who does that anymore? I thought all news was streaming. Anyway, she'd come out to retrieve her paper around the same time I'd be walking my dog. We'd wave. She oftentimes cycled at night around the same time I'd be walking the dog in the evening.

"She used to go down Slaters Lane to the Mount Vernon trail and bike into Old Town. Sometimes she'd return with some guy. They'd park their bikes and he'd spend the night. Normally that was on the weekend. Sometimes it was during the week."

There was more.

"Her mother visited her. The old lady lives right around the corner from Jane. Actually, I shouldn't call her an old lady. She and Jane look just like each another. People always confuse them. Hey, do you think it's possible someone wanted to kill her mother? Did you know they landed the helicopter right on Slaters Lane to take her to the hospital? Do you know her mother was taken to the hospital that same night? I'd never seen anything like that before. Everyone's still talking about it."

The video fizzled out. A second later, McCarthy called her. "Sorry," he said. "A transformer just blew in my neighborhood. A couple of blocks just lost electricity and internet. I guess it's one of the consequences of living during a lockdown."

"Oh, I know," Judkins said. "Where would we be without the internet? I couldn't do all my online stuff. I'd be lost. But the phone works. What else can I tell you?"

"You're doing pretty good for someone who doesn't pay any attention to her neighbors," McCarthy said. "What can you tell me about the guy on the bike?"

"What's to tell? It's hard to say what he looked like. He wore a bike helmet. I don't think I ever saw him when he wasn't wearing it. And that was the thing. He would return with her and they'd go inside, usually around the back of the house. It was like they didn't want to be seen together. Sometimes I thought he was a married man. He was well-built, physical, athletic, you know. You could tell from the racing clothes.

"I believe they had a rendezvous point somewhere along the Mount Vernon Trail or in Old Town. If you go down Slaters Lane, you know, across Washington Street and down toward the power plant, you can get onto the bike trail. It takes you along the edge of Old Town. I once followed her down there."

What's to tell? Indeed, thought McCarthy. "You followed her?"

"Listen, I don't want to make myself a witness or anything when they catch the son of a bitch who attacked her, but I was a little curious about that man. So one Saturday, when she went on a bike ride, I ran to my car and drove into Old Town. I got onto North Patrick and turned down Madison, which intersects with the bike path by the river. No sooner did I get there then I saw her coming along the path. Are you familiar with that part of Old Town?"

Judkis did not wait for an answer. She was just catching her breath. "Anyway, Madison is at the edge of Rivergate City Park. I saw her stop and meet the guy there. They chatted briefly. No hugs or kisses, which was a little strange and only confirmed my belief that these were clandestine meetings. They looped around and headed back up the trail toward Tide Lock Park and Slaters Lane. I didn't follow them. I went to King Street and bought myself an ice cream cone."

McCarthy jotted down a few notes. "I'd like to be able to interview the guy. He might be connected to her attack."

"You think so?" she asked, excitedly. She suddenly stopped talking. Then she said, "Listen, I don't want to get myself into any trouble or anything, but I did a little detective work myself about that guy. This was before she was attacked. I visited her house."

"When?"

"On Easter Sunday," said Judkis. "Maybe an hour or two before she was attacked. I thought he'd still be there and that I'd catch them in the act. I was curious as hell to find out who he was because...." Her voice trailed off. "Am I in trouble?"

"No," McCarthy said.

"Good. I swear to you that I did not try to kill that woman or anything like that. You understand?"

"Yes."

"Okay. I'm going to tell you something else now. And this might actually be important." She paused. "I have to go to the bathroom," she said. "I usually take the phone with me but sometimes people are offended when they hear the toilet flush. I'll be right back." She put down the phone.

McCarthy ran over to his kitchen — Aquarius — and refilled his coffee. He was back in his seat when she returned.

"Sorry," she said. "Where was I? I'm pretty sure I saw them together on Saturday, around dusk. They came back up from the trail, like they always do. I knew the routine. And I never saw him leave later in the evening. I was pretty sure he was still at the house. So Sunday I went over and knocked on her door."

She was repeating herself but McCarthy didn't interrupt. She went round and round for about ten minutes. Finally, he asked. "What time was it when you went to her place?"

"Around 1 p.m. About two hours before all hell broke loose with ambulances screaming down the street and that helicopter landing right in the middle of Slaters Lane. Anyway, I brought a potted plant with me. She was surprised. He was there. I saw him for an instant. He was leaving. It seemed to me that they had argued or something."

She anticipated his next question and added, "I didn't see him long enough or clearly enough to make an ID. I don't recall whether or not he was wearing glasses. Or if he had facial hair. I've been asking myself those questions since Monday. Listen, I don't want to get involved in this. I really don't."

He remained silent. It was not going to be possible to keep her out of the case, despite her desires. Unless someone else was arrested for the crime in the coming days, the man on the bike was a person of interest and needed to be identified and questioned.

"I liked Jane," Judkis said. "She had a certain vulnerability. I think she had a hard time finding the right man." She lowered her voice. "She fucked a lot of guys, if you don't mind my French. I saw the men come and go. But a long-term relationship wasn't her thing. Some people are blessed in that regard, like me. I've got a steady guy who's always at my side. I know how to keep them close at hand. I don't think she cared about that. She probably liked the lockdown."

McCarthy didn't say anything. Again, he let her talk. And talk. Finally, he interrupted and said, "Was that the *something else* you were going to tell me?"

"No. Yes."

McCarthy expected her to go to the bathroom again. Instead, she said, "The *something else* is that the guy on the bike was also seeing her mother, Tricia Barton. You don't have to ask me if I'm sure. I'm positive. I got more and more curious, so I followed him one day when he left Jane's place.

"Instead of taking Patrick to Madison, I drove down Bashford Lane. I almost ran into him. I expected him to head into Old Town but, instead, he went onto North Royal and stopped at Tricia Barton's place."

"How did you know it was Barton's home?"

"I once followed her from Jane's place to see where she lived. I know, it's like I was snooping or something, but I'm really not that kind of a person. I basically don't care what my neighbors are doing.

I'm more of a 'live and let live' kind of person. I was just intrigued by Jane's mother. They dress the same, you know. They're like twins. I don't know which one imitates the other. Maybe it's a little bit of both. It's weird though. They even live in the same kind of house. Identical. If you stand outside her mother's home, it's like looking at a mirror reflection of Jane's place. Everything is reversed, you know.

"But it's the same. Two big, thin, long windows next to the front door; three windows across on the upper floor, with the same kind of drapes inside; a slate roof; the building is a pinkish brick, a very unusual and distinct color; the doors are painted some shade of purple or plum; so on and so on."

She caught herself. "You don't think this is strange, do you?" she asked.

"No, no, not at all. In fact, this is very useful information. I appreciate your sharing. I don't think it's odd at all that you took so much interest in their affairs."

"No, not that," she corrected him. "Don't you think it's weird, the similarities between the two women? Always imitating one another."

"Oh, yes, definitely. Very strange. What else can you tell me about what you saw?"

"Nothing. It was only that one time. He stopped there. I was shocked. I just kept driving because I didn't want him to see me and get suspicious. I never went by Mrs. Barton's house again. I was too busy just keeping tabs on Jane," she laughed.

"You know," she added, "you must be really good at pulling information out of people because I've never told anyone else about this. And I don't want to get involved, particularly if Jane Hutton dies. I don't want to get dragged into this thing. I don't want to go to the police station and look at a line-up. I don't even want to be shown photographs." She suddenly got emotional. "I do not want to be asked to identify anyone. I am terrible at that sort of thing. I would never forgive myself if I identified the wrong person and he got convicted of assaulting or killing her. Do you promise to keep me out of this?"

McCarthy sighed. "I can't. I'm not handling the investigation. It's being conducted by the police department. I'm simply helping collect information at this preliminary stage. I'm going to have to share your name with other people. I won't share the details of our conversation with anyone now, but the time may come when you're going to have to tell investigators about it."

"Do you know who's in charge of the investigation?"

"I don't. That's still going to be determined. Right now, they're just collecting information. I also think it's going to be impacted by whether or not Jane Hutton dies. If this thing turns into a murder investigation, it's going to take on a life of its own. It's pretty serious, as is. But it's looking like it's a domestic case, to be honest. I shouldn't be telling you this, but the absence of any forced entry suggests Jane knew her assailant and opened the door for that person to come inside her home."

"Tricia Barton," Judkis whispered.

"Hard to say, but it's beginning to look that way."

"Here's my theory," she said. "Mrs. Barton found out that the guy was seeing her daughter. She freaked out. She went to her daughter's house and killed her. It all fits together. In fact…"

"What?"

"….I might have seen Barton outside of Hutton's home. I think I did. But I don't want to get involved in this, okay. I don't want to be on the front page of *The Washington Post* exposed as the person who solved the case. You have to keep me out of this."

"I'm always checking my temperature in case I'm coming down with the coronavirus," she said. "I was in Old Town for St. Patrick's Day. I was up and down King Street at all the bars, hanging out with many of my friends. I'd been invited all over and made stops at a lot of watering holes. Have you been to that new beer garden on King?"

Mac said he had not been there yet.

"Getting back to Jane Hutton and Tricia Barton," she said, "do you know why they have different last names? I looked it up. Curious, you know. Anyway, Hutton is Tricia Barton's maiden name. See what I mean about both of them being sort of like the same person? It fits, doesn't it? Tricia divorced her husband, Stan Barton, a well-known developer. He was gay. Left her a rich woman. She never mentions the guy. She blazed her own way. Didn't need a helping hand from any man to get ahead. Weird woman, but admirable."

While she talked, Judkis ran her palm over her left cheek, then her forehead, and finally her right cheek.

*

"It's done. Don't hate me."

THE EMAIL message was only two sentences. Perhaps the author thought it was sufficiently ambiguous so as to be innocuous. In D.C. the adage went, "Never put in an email anything that you would be embarrassed to see in the media." In this case, the adage could also be applied to a court of law. This was not the sort of message you would want to see in the hands of a jury.

The recipient printed the text and placed it in a file. It was all there in black and white: the name of the sender, the name of the recipient, their respective email addresses, and the date and time of the message (Thursday, April 16th, 3 p.m.). In the hands of a competent prosecutor, it was a smoking gun. Add a few juicy details and a jury had enough information to condemn the perpetrator to death.

Examining the text, the recipient considered various interpretations. Perhaps an argument could be made that it pertained to ending an affair. *We're done. It's history. So sorry. Don't be angry. I had to end it, darling. It's best for both of us. It's best for the four of us.* Perhaps a reader might conclude it was about a business disagreement. *I've transferred my shares in the company to our competitor. I hope we can still get together for drinks this weekend.* Or maybe it was some sort of dramatic act of a personal nature. *I've always wanted to be a woman!* Of course, none of those options was convincing. "It's done" did not refer to pot roast. "Don't hate me" had nothing to do with missing the rent. It was a confirmation. There was no doubt about it. Those words — written in a distinct bold font, used by the author in routine correspondence all of the time — would be proof that one party had shared their complicity in the attack upon Jane Hutton.

But how did it implicate the recipient? After all, that was the real question, wasn't it? In the end, who cared whether or not the author fried? The important thing was self-preservation. The question was whether a prosecutor, judge, and jury would conclude the message was proof of the guilt of the recipient. And guilt for what offense? After all, there were always levels of culpability. Would the recipient be considered as a co-conspirator, namely as someone who knew about the plan all along and participated actively in carrying it out? Or would the recipient be viewed as less culpable, perhaps as an accomplice after the fact, namely as someone who learned about the deed after it had occurred and acted at that time to conceal or assist the perpetrator?

The person to whom the email was addressed continued to examine the text. And it began to look more and more like a hologram that changed shape as it was examined from other angles. Could it be read as banter? Or perhaps as false bravado? In the end, was it proof of anything?

One could speculate forever as to the meaning of words. Did they show motive? Intent? Degree of culpability? The simple fact remained that Jane Hutton was fighting for her life in the ICU. And it was beginning to look more likely that she was going to die. Mo Katz mentioned it privately to one of his associates, and word got around.

The recipient wondered what to do with the message. Should it be reported to the police now? If so, what would be said? *"I had nothing to do with this. We never discussed it. Okay, we did discuss it, but I never took those conversations seriously. Well, that's not entirely accurate. I did take it seriously but I honestly never thought the other party would carry through with it. No, in truth, I did. I thought the author of that note was entirely capable of killing Jane Hutton."* How would that come across? Probably not too well. The police wouldn't buy it. There would be an indictment and a trial. In the end, the testimony of the assailant would be a key factor. If the assailant testified that they had acted in concert, there wasn't a chance in hell that the accomplice would be acquitted. If, however, the assailant said it was undertaken without any involvement or encouragement from the other party, well, even then the jury would reject the testimony. The jury might conclude that the testimony was a fabrication to protect the other party. Bottom line: the confession of the perpetrator was going to determine the outcome for both of them.

All of these scenarios were maddening. This was insane. It was best not to think about all the different variations on the theme. Let it play out and see what happens. Maybe Hutton would die? Maybe the assailant would do something equally crazy and commit suicide. Maybe this, maybe that. The alternative sets of facts were off the charts. Suffice to say the tragedy was inevitable and inescapable. This was not a time to look back. One had to look forward. There had to be a way out of this without notifying the police at this time. When smart people get into trouble, they work their way through it. That would happen here. Some opportunity would avail itself. It was all about being attentive and seizing the opportunity when it presented itself.

*

THE EFFECTS of the coronavirus continued to impact the court. Before the week was over, all courtroom proceedings were shut down for at least two months. The announcement read:

All civil and criminal in-person proceedings in the U.S. District Court for the Eastern District of Virginia, including

court appearances, trials, hearings, settlement conferences, and naturalization ceremonies scheduled to occur through June 10, 2020, with the exception of critical or emergency proceedings, are POSTPONED, subject to the conditions set forth in this General Order.

The closures of the courts did not mean the system was grinding to a halt. Like everything else, it was adapting to the coronavirus and fighting to stay alive as the virus infected bodies and businesses. More video hearings were conducted each day by the court. And the U.S. Attorney's office was besieged with a rash of fraud cases inspired by the coronavirus.

The cases took a variety of forms, like the virus itself. Some people sought ways to fraudulently benefit from the $3 trillion the federal government was pumping into the economy to keep businesses, hospitals, and local governments afloat. Others resorted to hacking. Whether it was the passwords and usernames for bank accounts, employment or medical files, or personal email accounts, hackers were busy busting into accounts and stealing money or identities, causing unneeded grief and embarrassment to innocent parties during a stressful time.

The post-Katrina National Center for Disaster Fraud was deluged with nearly 10,000 tips of wrongdoing. Federal, state and local authorities scrambled to identify and stop scams appearing online, in the mail, and on the phone. DOJ and the FBI issued bulletins about people who were trying to take advantage of COVID-19. Some were peddling false remedies to the virus while others were filing false claims about contracting the virus or about family members dying from it. Still others were seeking to collect money from hospitals and clinics to ship nonexistent masks, gloves and other protective gear. Charges of hoarding, price gouging, kickbacks, and false claims were only some of the forms of fraud that appeared throughout the criminal justice system.

In a phone call with Katz, Lin couldn't hide her disgust about the current situation. "It's a sad commentary on life when people take advantage of a deadly virus to hawk their wares, and do so fraudulently. It's not enough for hospitals and clinics to compete against one another to get ventilators, protective masks, and other devices to save people and safeguard themselves. Now they have to worry about scammers. It's pretty pathetic."

He responded with wisdom born of experience. "It's been going on as long as man has walked the earth. There are always going to be people trying to make a buck any way they can, whether it's legal or illegal. I concur with your sentiment. But the job of everyone in our office is to try to stave this activity and protect innocent parties during the pandemic. As soon as our investigation into the circumstances surrounding Jane's attack is finished, I'll assign you to one of the task forces dealing with fraud. They will benefit from your expertise and commitment."

In addition to investigations into fraudulent activities, attorneys and investigators in the office were assisting local police departments throughout the D.C. area with sting operations directed at sexual predators who preyed on children. At least one of those operations was going to be made public by the end of the week. Katz directed several of his attorneys to track complaints that came directly to his office. Attorneys were assigned to DOJ and regional task forces. Still others participated in video conferences about schemes that were impacting the entire D.C. region.

Although his resources were spread thin, he wanted to keep his most trusted team fully engaged in the Hutton case. He knew it was only a matter of time before someone registered a complaint that he was diverting federal resources to assist in a local prosecution, despite the fact that the victim was one of his own employees.

The moment arrived more quickly than expected. On Friday, he received an email from Ryan Long, an investigator in the Office of the Inspector General. Katz could not fault him. Just as he and his attorneys were fighting fraud occurring in the public sector, the OIG and other internal units were responding to complaints about federal employees using drugs and abusing alcohol, taking advantage of telework schedules to perform chores around their houses, and earning income from outside sources while collecting an unemployment paycheck.

Long's email read: "It has come to our attention that the Office of the U.S. Attorney for the Eastern District of Virginia (hereinafter referred to as "the Office") has been diverting resources and personnel from the roles and responsibilities assigned to this office to assist the investigation of an assault that occurred within the confines of the City of Alexandria. The assault case does not fall under the jurisdiction of the Office. The City of Alexandria's Police Department is uniquely positioned to investigate all aspects of this matter. Involvement by the Office in the affairs of a local municipality's police function could unduly prejudice the prosecution of the matter and constitutes a gross misallocation of Federal resources. The Office is not authorized to involve itself in such a matter. I request that any and all work cease immediately. I request the names, titles, and pertinent contact information of all individuals whose time and effort are currently being diverted from the needs of the Office to the city's investigation. This information should be provided to my office no later than close of business today."

As Katz read the email, his phone rang. He checked the number and glanced at Long's contact information. The 202 number was the same. He did not answer the phone. He finished reading the email and deleted it, and then went to his delete folder and permanently erased the email from his files. His phone vibrated that a message had just been recorded. He checked it. The message was as follows: "Mr. Katz, this is Ryan Long from the IG's office. I sent you an email a few moments ago. Please call me to acknowledge receipt of the email and indicate that you will comply with it." He deleted the message from his phone too.

He reflected on the email from Long. Nowhere did it

acknowledge that the assault was against one of his two deputies. He wondered who would file a complaint and why it was being acted upon so quickly. Someone, he concluded, wanted him and his team off the case.

As he pondered the situation, his phone rang again. He recognized the number and picked up. "Hey, Sally," he said. It was Sally Orr, a 20-year veteran of the office. In her capacity as a senior civil litigator, she was picking up the slack in Hutton's absence. Katz had bypassed her selecting Hutton as deputy of the civil division. Katz knew she was disappointed, but she never complained.

"Sir, I need your counsel about an issue that's percolating up in the civil branch. We're getting lots of calls from restaurants and regular Main Street businesses asking us to file charges against insurance companies who are refusing claims related to the coronavirus. I'm not sure how you want us to proceed."

"What's the issue?" Civil cases were never Katz's forte. He handled some while he was in private practice, but primarily because they were more lucrative than his criminal defense practice and he used the income generated by those cases to devote time to the cases he loved, primarily defending misdemeanants who lacked the finances to afford his standard fees.

"There's a lot of contention about whether 'business interruption' claims should be honored in insurance policies during the coronavirus. The insurance carriers are claiming that they have specific exemptions for viruses. The Main Street businesses claim that a blanket exemption like that should not be enforced. The state and federal politicians are all over the place, basically taking whichever side historically provided more money to their reelection bids. It is true that most policies have specific exemptions for pandemics and viruses. But there's a fairly strong argument that can be made for the other side."

Katz thought about it for a minute and asked, "What do you think?"

"I think we should stay out of it for now, sir, and tell the businesses that we're going to leave it to civil remedies without intruding on either side. The way I see it, we should just let them battle it out in court. Several lawsuits have already been filed by mom-and-pop companies seeking damages against insurance carriers. It'll sort itself out, and we don't need to get in the middle of it."

"That sounds right, Sally. Let's take that approach." Before he ended the call, Katz said, "Sally, how's it going in the civil branch? You're a veteran. Are people handling the caseload? I've diverted a few of our resources to help with the investigation of Jane's attack. Are people okay with that decision?"

"Seriously, sir?" she asked. "I mean, people are wildly supportive of your action. Everyone says it shows that you have our interests at heart. There's been no negative impact caused by diverting resources. Your comments hit home. We are privileged to be drawing a paycheck, like you said on Monday. This is the worst economy since the Great Depression. Millions of people are unemployed. We've redoubled our effort and it's going to continue for the duration. I think most of us would favor Mai Lin, Mac and Curtis working alongside the Alexandria police department until this case is solved. They're an awesome team. We want the person responsible for harming Jane taken into custody. I'm actually surprised you're asking. Has something happened?"

"Nothing's happened," Katz replied. "I was just curious."

Orr wasn't buying it. "May I speak freely, sir? If someone is complaining about how we're helping the police, I'd tell them to F off. Anyway, that's my two cents."

Katz laughed and said he appreciated her candor. After the call ended, he thought about Long's email again and tried to divine where the complaint had originated. He now regretted deleting the communication from his system. Then he remembered that there was a way to retrieve a deleted email. He contacted Lin to walk him through the process. He found the email and studied it dispassionately for the first time. He concluded that Long had not written the email. It was too formal and rigid. Rather, Katz concluded, it was written by the person who lodged the complaint.

Long might have forwarded the email to Katz as a personal favor to someone else, Katz surmised. If that was true, then the IG might not have actually launched an investigation. He wondered if he could find any emails in his records that might mirror the tone of Long's email. Who did he know who wrote like that? He scoured files. It took about an hour, but he found what he was looking for, namely an email that included a lot of the same verbiage that Long had used.

The phrases "roles and responsibilities," "unduly prejudice," and "gross misallocation of Federal resources" were hardly unique, but having all three of them appear in two unrelated emails was hardly coincidental. It was not definitive evidence that the same person had written both pieces of correspondence. Yet it confirmed a suspicion that had been lurking in the back of Katz's head since Sunday afternoon.

*

IN THE EVENING, Snowe reported that toilet paper was rumored to have been spotted at the Safeway on N. Royal Street, so Katz made a TP run. He drove down King Street. All of the stores were closed, with the exception of a few eateries. Katz wondered what would happen to them. Would everyone go bankrupt in the end? Was it possible that the coronavirus was not a V-shaped curve or a "swoosh," but a horrible flushing sound that carried down the entire economy?

As he mused about the effects of this silent enemy, he drove by one of the two wig shops on King Street. Those stores had been in Old Town forever. He always wondered how they managed to stay in business. Now the window displays appeared incongruous with the world on the other side of the glass. Here were all these mannequins placed next to one another, each with a wig on its head. No six feet of separation for them in the store window. People peering into the shop stood six feet apart, but each of these mannequins was practically kissing the mannequin beside it, either on the cheek or the ear. He thought it would be amusing to place protective masks on a few of them. But then, he thought, if someone had a protective mask to spare, it should be donated to a hospital or healthcare worker rather than used to dress up a mannequin.

He stopped in the Safeway parking lot and went inside. The rumor was true. He picked up one eight-roll container. Let others have a chance to get some too. No hoarding, he thought. Katz had always been amazed at the variety of products in grocery stores, but tonight he felt something other than amazement. It was gratitude, and the shelves were half empty.

He tossed the rolls of toilet paper in the backseat and returned home by the same route he had taken to the grocery store. Driving through the same empty streets with darkened store fronts, he wondered what the future held for him. How might his job change? What effect would the coronavirus have upon efforts to reduce the number of people incarcerated for criminal offenses? The U.S. had the world's largest inmate population. Approximately 2 million people were incarcerated in America, with another 6 million on probation and parole. A disproportionate number of them were people of color. Despite all of the talk about reducing imprisonment, the reductions had not been substantial in the past few years. Maybe that would change because of COVID-19. What impact would the coronavirus have upon the jury system, the bedrock of jurisprudence? Would people be disinclined to sit on juries and confer with one another in closed quarters about the guilt or innocence of parties accused of serious crimes?

Katz also wondered what his personal life would be like in a post-coronavirus world. He had planned to step down as U.S. Attorney in another year or so, provided he was not removed beforehand for political reasons. But truth be told, he had a level of financial protection as a federal employee that was unavailable to his brethren in private practice. Some of them were earning no income while others were earning only a fraction of their normal salary. He was earning his full salary and it would continue unaffected by the consequences of the virus. That financial security was worth considering before he relinquished a government job.

Katz thought about where things were headed. Right now there were multiple unknowns. No one knew if the disease would peter out or return with the next flu season. Still unknown was whether people built immunities if they survived the infection, or whether the virus would mutate and seek out children and women the way it currently seemed to prefer older men.

And what about his personal life? He wondered whether his mother would survive the coronavirus. He didn't know how she was tonight. She might be in an induced coma with a tube stuck down her throat, lying beside a ventilator in a hospital filled with others who were dead and dying. And where was his father? Was he semi-delirious worrying about her or was he sitting in the living room blissfully remembering their golden years? Then his thoughts leapfrogged to his relationship with Abby Snowe. Where was that headed? Did they want to start a family after seeing the pain and anguish that could be unleashed by a virus?

Katz walked to his house after parking a block away. On the way he passed a couple who glanced at him enviously. He had scored TP. When he got to the house, he heard Snowe call him. He was just in time. Could he come upstairs? she asked. And could he bring a roll of toilet paper with him?

*

AS KATZ's TEAM worked, they remained in constant contact with one another. It allowed them to cross-pollinate information, share leads, and keep their morale from flagging. McCarthy placed a video call to Lin. "How's it going?" he asked. "Tell me some good news. I'm basically going in circles. I hope you're making progress. Where are you looking for stuff?"

"I've been doing some research on the chairman of BOM, Suzanne Marconi," she said. "It turns out she had a grudge against Jane for pleading to the criminal count in last year's settlement. According to Marconi's administrative assistant, she flew off the handle when the settlement was announced and wanted Jane fired. Late last year, BOM terminated its relationship with Stephens Babcock."

McCarthy was hunched over on the screen, his chin resting on his hand. His expression was blank.

"Did you know that, Mac?" Lin asked. "You don't seem surprised."

"Quite the opposite," he replied. "I'm shocked. I can't imagine Jane would have settled any case without the client's permission. That doesn't make any sense. But even if she failed to tell this Marconi person, is Marconi really going to be so enraged that she tries to murder Jane?

"To me, the murderer is someone close to Jane. I feel it in my bones. Boyfriend. Mother. Close friend. That's who I'm focused on. I don't buy the possibility that it was someone on an outer ring."

"Remember what Mo told us," Lin cautioned. "He said anyone is capable of doing anything under the right set of circumstances. Suspect everyone. Discount no one."

"Out of curiosity, where does Marconi live?" McCarthy asked.

"In D.C. on Foxhall Road."

McCarthy whistled. "That's a pretty swanky part of town. No one would come that distance to attack Jane, particularly with the coronavirus raging. People aren't leaving their homes. It's not her. The assailant lives close by."

Lin was getting irritated. "When you outlined the case for us, you said that it was probably done by a woman," she said. "In addition, you implied that there might have been something simmering in the relationship between the victim and perpetrator that manifested itself as soon as Jane opened the door. Anger over the settlement surely marks that box."

Lin had more information. "Plus, I did a little more digging into Ms. Marconi. I contacted D. Shorter, the IT guy. He got Jane's phone records for me. It turns out Marconi called Jane twice last week. The first call was on Wednesday, the 8th, and the second on Friday, the 10th. Jane did not answer either call. Marconi left a message after the second call."

"And?"

"I listened to it. Marconi was cagey. She didn't scream or anything. But she did threaten Jane. It's subtle, but it's a threat. I've got it here." McCarthy could see Lin clicking keys on her laptop. "Give me a second and I'll send it over. Okay, I just sent it. It's pretty long. Let me know what you think after you listen to it."

A second later, McCarthy acknowledged receipt. He immediately opened the link and played the recording.

"Jane, this is Suzanne Marconi. This is uncomfortable. One of my employees in Richmond is leveling allegations against Simon. She's threatening to file a complaint of some sort. I've been told it could be sent to your office. If it does, please don't take any precipitous action. The allegations are spurious. Now I don't expect you to take my word for it. I know you hate Simon and that you'd love to nail him. Plus, there's no love lost between you and me. But please don't take what she says at face value. Simon is a good man, despite how things ended up between the two of you. Any action on your part is retaliation, as far as I'm concerned. If you want war, you'll get it. Both inside and outside of the courtroom. People die on the battlefield; bodies are carried off on stretchers. I'm not threatening you but I'll do everything in my power to make sure you rue the day.

He played it twice more. Then he asked Lin, "Who is Simon and what's the connection between Simon and Marconi? Did Jane ever receive a complaint? If so, who filed it? What's this line about retaliation? And do you really think Marconi is threatening Jane? I mean, she says she isn't. It sounds to me like a lot of false bravado."

"All good questions," she said. "I can look into it."

"Don't knock yourself out," McCarthy said. "In the end, this isn't going to be about Suzanne Marconi. Mark my words. It's about someone who lived in close proximity to Jane Hutton. The attacker is right under our noses.

"You've got a lot on your plate. If you want, I can track down more information about this complaint. If you want to do research on Simon, you might look at Hank Simon. He used to be an item with Jane's mother."

"How do you know that?"

"It used to be a regular item in the gossip column in the *Post*." He paused before asking,

"Where else are you looking for clues?"

"Nowhere, actually," she replied.

After the call ended, Lin made some tea and then engrossed herself in work. Her life consisted of feeding and playing with her son, eating, sleeping, and conducting research. It was repetitive. There was no schedule. She was operating in a zone where there was no time and no space. It was weird, losing track of time.

She Googled Hank Simon. She had never heard of him. Yet there he was sandwiched between Mark Zuckerberg and Larry Ellison as among the richest people in the U.S. The list ran as follows:

Jeff Bezos, Amazon – $114 billion.

Bill Gates, Microsoft – $106 billion.

Warren Buffett, Berkshire Hathaway – $80.8 billion.

Mark Zuckerberg, Facebook – $69.6 billion.

Hank Simon, GlassGrass – $67 billion.

Larry Ellison, software – $65 billion.

Larry Page, Google – $55.5 billion.

Sergey Brin, Google – $53.5 billion.

Excited, she called McCarthy. She felt she was onto something. He did not answer. Lin was disappointed but concluded he was entitled to a few hours of rest and relaxation. They were all working around the clock. She then called Santana. He answered. She explained the situation, played the recording, and told Santana about Hank Simon. "He's a bloody billionaire," she said. "The head of an eco-friendly fiber optics conglomerate. I never heard of it. But it's huge."

"Huge doesn't adequately describe it," said Santana, who was familiar with the Fortune 100 Company. "They have contracts with DOJ and U.S. Attorney's offices, as well as the Pentagon. That company is unrivaled. It destroys the competition. In fact, it's involved in a contested contract now. Do you know what I'm talking about? GlassGrass lost the bid for some multi-billion-dollar contract and is claiming undue political influence."

She looked up GlassGrass. It had a major presence in D.C. She knew that Washington was a prime feeding ground for tech, defense, and other companies seeking billions of dollars in contracts from congressional appropriations. The action would only become more intense as Congress authorized trillions this month to combat COVID-19.

Amazon was building its HQ2 opposite I-395 from the Pentagon. Boeing had a large corporate presence around the corner at the edge of Crystal City. GlassGrass was building a major facility in Potomac Yard next to the new Metro station under construction.

"I just found something," Lin said. "A connection between Marconi and Simon. He's on the board of BOM. He joined at the beginning of 2020."

"Okay," Santana said, connecting the dots based upon the information in front of him. "Marconi wanted to stop a federal prosecutor from inquiring into a member of BOM's board. I can see how the inquiry might create further bad publicity and controversy for the company. But I'm surprised that Hank Simon is the subject of a complaint. He's squeaky clean. Not the sort to be the subject of a whistleblower complaint."

"I understand," Lin said. "Mac said I was barking up the wrong tree."

With that, the call ended.

Lin climbed down the spiral staircase from her makeshift office in the loft to the bedroom below. Reese was fast asleep. She went to the bathroom. She studied her face in the mirror, looking at the circles under her eyes. Maybe she was barking up the wrong tree, as McCarthy had said. A moment later, she tiptoed into the baby's room and watched him sleeping. He was cherubic, oblivious to everything swirling around in the world outside. There was a deadly virus. There were vicious and horrible people. But in the face of a baby asleep in a warm bed, Lin saw love and hope.

*

KATZ COULD not shake a feeling of dread. Despite some trepidation, he finally completed a call after dialing the same number and hanging up several times. "Hey, Pops, it's Mo." He said. "How are you?"

"I'm fine, son. I had a sense you were thinking about me tonight. I'm fine. I miss your mother. I haven't heard anything. I was watching the news tonight. I saw a piece about a bunch of bodies they kept in a large cooler outside of the hospital. I didn't see your mother among them." He chuckled. "I've got to find some humor in all of this, you know. Otherwise, I think I'd go crazy." He paused, and Katz could hear him taking a deep breath. "I miss your mom," he said, his voice cracking. "I'm lost, son."

"It's going to be alright," Katz said. "I have faith, Pops. The most important thing right now is simply to remain positive. You have to believe mom is going to survive. That's all we can do." He hesitated. "She's not on a ventilator yet, right?"

"Not so far as I know," said his father.

*

"WHAT IS IT?" Lin asked. It was midnight. Reese was standing by the window in the bedroom. A nightlight from the adjoining baby's room spread a faint ray of light across the hallway and into their room, displaying Reese in stark relief. He was brooding. "What's going on?"

"I never hide anything," Reese began. "That was the vow we made to each another. You get to know everything about me, past and present. I've never tried to be anything less than totally transparent with you."

Lin was perplexed. She knew David was faithful. He wasn't the sort of man to cheat on her. She knew he was honest with their finances and their dealings with friends and neighbors. Although she never said it to him, she thought he shared too much information about his background and growing up. It was more than she shared with him. People were entitled to some secrets. If you eliminated all the mystery, you might lose the attraction, she thought. "Have you gotten yourself into some kind of trouble?" she asked.

"It has to do with Sherry Stone. She shared something with me. It's about Jane Hutton. I promised not to tell anyone. But it's creating a tension inside of me. Sherry knows things that she isn't sharing with Mo and the rest of you. I'm not sure what she's doing."

Lin got up and stood beside him. Reese was getting agitated and she didn't want him to wake the baby. "Keep your voice down, David," she instructed. She held his hand. "Do you distrust her?"

"She's different. She's got an edge. She never lets you feel entirely comfortable around her. I like that about her, but it's also the thing that makes me nervous. It's not that I distrust her, exactly. It's more like I question her technique, if that makes sense to you."

"Come to bed," Lin said, patting the mattress. She sat down on the edge of the bed. Reese sat beside her. "You feel like you're betraying me and the others on the team, is that it?" she asked. The silhouette nodded. She moved away and propped herself up against the headboard. "If Sherry told you to keep something a secret, you should honor her request. You might question her methods, but I don't. If you remember, she and Mo captured the man responsible for that double murder last year, including the body found at Jones Point. I watched the way Mo relied on her every step of the way.

"You know I try to emulate Mo. If he trusts her, then I trust her. All she really wants to do is catch the person responsible for hurting Jane Hutton. It's her way of getting to the truth. If she's not sharing certain information, there's a good reason for it.

"Don't break your promise to her. I'll never hold it against you. In fact, the only thing I would be angry about is if you told me. Okay? Now come to bed."

He crawled into bed beside her. They held one another, and Reese sighed deeply. Lin had a feeling that Sherry Stone was pursuing a line of inquiry that led to the truth. There was nothing to worry about. It would all reveal itself in good time.

*

SANTANA AWOKE in the middle of the night. He slipped out of bed, checked to be sure he had not disturbed Stone, and went downstairs. His circadian rhythm was disrupted by the coronavirus. It made little difference what time he got up in the morning anymore. So what if he stayed up all night working on a case, he thought.

He fired up his computer and examined Hutton's records from her old firm. When he and Stone first looked at those cases, they saw different patterns and reached divergent conclusions. He saw Hutton as a white knight pursuing justice against parties who had committed wrongful acts, while Stone believed Hutton was shaking down those parties for her personal gain. The thought that woke him up was the possibility that there might be a third explanation, a hybrid between the two extremes. If he was right, then both he and Stone were partially correct in their interpretation.

As Stone had reminded him, Hutton could not adopt the role of a caped crusader. It was impermissible for an attorney to use a client's confidential information. Secrets were sacrosanct. Information shared in the confidence of a law office stayed there forever. If a corporate client was acquitted of a crime it had committed, that was a 'win' for both the company and for the firm that represented it. It was ludicrous to imagine Hutton would seek redress against former clients who had "gotten off" for wrongdoing. Marvel action heroes might right societal wrongs, but it wasn't the job of lawyers.

But Stone's theory was equally flawed. Watching Hutton the past six months, Santana saw that she adhered to impeccable ethical standards. She would never be involved in a scheme to shake down a client by threatening to expose their past wrongdoings. True, he might not be able to detect everything about everyone with whom he came into contact, but he was pretty sure he had Hutton pegged right. She was honest to her core.

The gnawing feeling that awoke him in the middle of the night was the possibility that Hutton was attacked because someone was threatened by something in those records.

He texted Lin to contact him in the morning. She had just finished feeding her baby and was placing him in his crib when her phone vibrated. She left the baby's room, headed to the kitchen to make a cup of decaffeinated tea, and glanced at the phone.

"What's up?" she texted back.

"Did Jane have any cases in our office that involved clients of her old firm?"

"Yes. Why?"

"Jane was tracking someone. I'm trying to figure out what it was. There could be answers in those files."

Lin stepped outside onto the patio of her top floor apartment in the three-story building. It overlooked a courtyard of townhomes with postage-sized backyards enclosed by wooden fences. In the distance, a dog was barking. The sky was sprinkled with stars. Three of them were shining brightly. She put in a call to Santana, who answered immediately.

"It's complicated," she said. "But, first, what do you know about stars? There are these really bright stars out here tonight. They're like lights strung on a cord."

"I know that Jupiter, Saturn and Mars are out there tonight and that they form an arc on the ecliptic. Don't ask me how I know that. I read it somewhere. Why? Are you outside?"

"Yes. I don't want to wake the baby. What's an ecliptic?"

"I have no idea," Santana laughed. "I just remember reading about it. I also read that everything happening to us right now can be explained by those three planets being in alignment. Probably some crazy-ass astrology." He laughed again. "What can you tell me about those cases?"

"After she came onboard, Jane informed me that she had brought a thumb drive with her from Stephens Babcock. She gave it to me for safekeeping. It's in my credenza at the office. I'll have to retrieve it one of these days, but I'm not going back to the office for the time being.

"She did not want anyone to know about it. I'm not sure why she wanted people kept in the dark, but I didn't say anything."

"Did Sally Orr know about it? She's the number two in the civil division."

"No, Curtis. Like I told you, she told me not to discuss it with anyone."

Santana wondered about Orr. She had every right to begrudge Hutton. Katz had passed over Orr when he named Hutton to head the civil branch of the office. Regardless of the qualifications that Hutton brought to the job, many of the attorneys believed Katz acted insensitively. Orr never complained, but that was not a reason to discount her as a suspect. Sometimes it was the people you least expected who did the most outlandish things, and that included murder.

"Where does Sally live?" Santana asked.

"Oh, please, Curtis," Lin replied. "There is no way she would have harmed Jane. She was protective toward everyone and everything in the office. She's like the perfect public servant." She paused and then added, "She lives in Old Town. About six blocks from Slaters Lane, on Alfred Street. I've been to her house a couple of times to drop off files."

"Okay," Santana said. "Out of curiosity, do you know whether Hutton had any dealings with any clients from her old firm in the past six months?"

"I don't think so," Lin said. "Jane occasionally emailed attorneys from her old firm, but I don't think she ever reached out to old clients. All of those emails should be in our files. Jane was very meticulous about maintaining a thorough electronic paper trail."

He made a note to check it in the days ahead. "Was there anything that Jane ever said to you that might shed some light on why she took files from her old firm and put them on a thumb drive?" he asked.

Lin thought for a minute. "Jane once told me the files showed the *modus operandi* of a particular individual and that it was only a matter of time before he resurfaced and committed new crimes using the same methodology. She wanted to be ready to nab that individual the next go around."

"That jives with what I'm thinking," Santana said. "We need to get back to the office sooner rather than later and check the records in that thumb drive."

Lin leaned over the railing and looked up at the sky. The night was dark and clear. As her eyes became accustomed to the night, she saw more and more stars. She heard the tea kettle beginning to whistle. She went inside and turned off the burner.

Santana said, "I hope nobody in our office is involved in Jane's attack."

Lin placed a tea bag in a cup and filled it with hot water. "Can you hold on for a second?" she asked. Taking the cup in one hand, and

105

holding the phone in the other, she returned outside and continued the conversation. "I think there may have been some jealousy toward Jane by others in the office, not because she was promoted over Sally Orr necessarily but because she was just a little smarter and a little better than everyone else. Some people resent that. But I can't believe it would lead anyone to attack her." Lin sat in one of two chairs on the deck, putting the teacup on a side table. Then she turned on the speakerphone and opened an app to conduct a search. "That's just too crazy to contemplate."

"I hope you're right," Santana said. "I'll let you go. If you have a chance, dig around and see whether you can find anything more about the case involving one of our attorneys. I'd be curious to know if it's Sally Orr."

"Okay," Lin said. "And, by the way, it's the pathway of the sun and moon across the sky."

"What is?"

"The ecliptic." She looked up. The stars shone across the sky like shiny pieces of glass scattered across a black abyss. She believed there was a God and that God was good. Why then were so many people dying from the coronavirus? Two thousand a day in the U.S. alone. Why did a merciful and loving God allow that to happen? She felt small and insignificant staring up at the heavens. She also felt empowered. She and David had formed a nucleus and together they had started a family. By her actions, she was fighting against virus, infestation, famine, flood and every other disaster that existed in the universe. The stars twinkled at her and she gazed back.

Chapter Two: ORR

IN THE MORNING, Katz called Shorter. "Do you retain copies of video conference calls?" he asked. "I want to watch the ones in which Jane Hutton participated."

"I may have files on some of them, though I doubt it," Shorter answered. "I don't see how videos of conference calls are going to help you find the person who did this to her."

"When we conduct the calls, everyone is in their homes," Katz explained. "Jane had her computer set up in her kitchen. She participated in all the calls with the computer at exactly the same angle. There were kitchen counters behind her. I want to study the background and see if there are any clues related to the attack.

"I want to study her, too. Sometimes people say things that seem irrelevant but are dripping with significance when you go back and hear them afterwards. Sometimes people tell you things by the way they're dressed or by their expressions. I know I'm reaching for straws, D. But it's the only thing I got."

"It makes sense now that you explain it," Shorter said. "It's like looking at photos. Seeing a room inside her house is like visiting it before the incident occurred. You might see something that evaded the forensic crew. I'll pull our tapes and see what's what.

"We definitely keep copies of computer communications, including documents, telephone conversations, emails, text messages, and the like. No one has ever inquired about records of video conferences. To be honest, no one was using our video conferencing capability until everyone started teleworking."

Katz gave Shorter his private number. "Call me any if you find anything," he said. Katz stepped outside onto the brick patio behind his townhouse. Leaves on the trees had unfurled like flags. Birds zoomed in and out of bushes. Squirrels imitated circus acrobats as they walked along the top of the wooden backyard fence or leapt from tree to tree. Now that he was home during the day, he saw things he never noticed before. It was a far cry from days spent walking between floors in the office and courthouse. In fact, he could have sworn he'd seen a fox streak through the yard the other day, although it moved so fast he wasn't sure whether it was a fox or a figment of his imagination.

Katz had read that goats were retaking some village in Wales and wondered if wildlife had noticed that humans were no longer venturing outside. What did birds, squirrels, and foxes make of this new normal? And what about pollution? Maybe ice would start reforming on the Arctic cap. Was it conceivable that environmentalists would encourage the burning of fossil fuels to reverse a cooling pattern on earth? Perhaps that was far-fetched, but there was no doubt there would be profound changes in all aspects of life. Plus, it felt abnormally cool this April.

Katz thought about the new normal writ large. What was it going to be like when they emerged from the pandemic? Things would never return to the way they were before the crisis. More people would telework; fewer would commute. Perhaps people would move out of heavily congested cities to smaller towns.

And what about the world of criminal justice? There would probably be a greater push against incarceration and toward home detention. More court proceedings would be heard remotely, particularly motions about the constitutionality of searches and seizures. From this point forward, police would be reluctant to stop speeding motorists or people on the sidewalk committing minor crimes.

"What are you thinking?" Snowe asked, joining him outside. She had taken a break from her telework as a probation officer for the City of Alexandria. She faced a unique set of problems in her job. Many of her clients came from families who did not own computers. She was only able to accomplish a portion of her work indoors. The remainder involved going outdoors and visiting youngsters on probation in their homes. When she traveled, she wore a protective mask and gloves.

"I'm thinking that we're living through something as profound as World War II or the Black Death," he said. "It's a seminal moment in history, unlike anything you or I have experienced in our lifetime. Something that historians are going to write about for hundreds of years to come. It's going to be important to see what we do as we come out of this thing. I don't think we go back to the way things were before. If nothing else, people are going to maintain social distancing and that means our entire world is going to undergo some radical changes."

"Thank God the internet came along when it did," she said. "We'd be lost without it." They received their news online and conducted all their business on their computers and tablets, including banking. He imagined how revolting it would be if they had to touch cash. "Speaking of which, want to go shopping?" she asked.

"Where?"

"Online. I want to visit an online hardware store and get a few items. You can push the cart up and down the aisles," he said, grinning at her.

Together they spent an hour ordering the hardware supplies, meats from one grocer, fruits and vegetables from another, and dairy from a third. "We'll have to make some bread later this week," she said. "It's pretty hard to find anything online. Oh, and if you haven't already started skimping on toilet paper, start now. One square a day should do it. That four pack from Safeway isn't going to last forever." He nodded but looked doubtful. "Actually, I've been looking at bidets online," Snowe said. "Solves the TP problem."

"Well, if you buy one, get a plumber to install it," he said. He was useless around the house when it came to plumbing and electrical work. His expertise was in lounging and making coffee.

*

THE NEXT email arrived just soon after the first one. What was

109

she thinking? This was the most incriminating evidence imaginable. People would immediately realize that she had acted on her own.

"**I'm sorry for sending you such a curt email. It was cruel to tell you it's done without further explanation. I will provide it the next time we meet. When will you visit? Say 10 pm tonight? The front door will be open. I regret my actions. I was rash and hysterical. Now I am afraid. I appreciate your exercising discretion and not sharing my previous communication with the police. I don't want to get you in the middle of this. If it has to come out, I will take full responsibility. I feel I acted in both our best interests. Until tonight, affectionately yours.**"

There was no need for a further explanation after sending an email that stated, "It's done." The lack of any further explanation would have been fine. It was preferred. Now the cracks were filling in. And a request that he visit? That was insane. He would not come to her home under any circumstances. Even though it was only across Old Town, it was dangerous to do so. He had the perfect out, of course. Travel was discouraged. He couldn't visit even if he wanted to. (And he didn't!) He was abiding by the governor's instructions. Though it was nice for her to express regret about putting him in the middle of things. Hopefully his attorney would draw the jury's attention to that particular detail before they decided to send him to jail. She was an intelligent woman but she was acting like a complete fool. It was only a matter of time before the floor caved in beneath him. He always knew this was going to happen.

*

KATZ AND HIS TEAM conducted a video call with Stone. They had been working the case for a week. Hutton's condition had worsened. In addition to recovering from her injuries, she had contracted the coronavirus. No one was surprised to learn that news. Tricia Barton was said to be making preliminary plans for her daughter's funeral. Against this backdrop, the desire to find the perpetrator grew stronger.

Each staffer filled a separate box on Katz's computer screen. Santana wore a cap and T-shirt. Lin held her baby, who was sleeping. Reese was seated beside her. The background displayed on McCarthy's screen was new. He had moved from Aquarius to Odyssey. The view of planet earth was about the same. His computer rested on top of two old volumes of Encyclopedia Britannica that he had inherited from his parents, who had purchased the encyclopedias for him as a youngster only to see them replaced with an online version in a couple of years. Katz had his computer on the dining room table. He wore a microfiber pullover with a T-shirt underneath. Stone was dressed in a black turtleneck and large gold hoop earrings that dangled to her broad shoulders.

Each party reported on their progress. McCarthy went first. "I've had a series of video chats with people who live in the neighborhood around Slaters Lane," he said. "There are some strange people in this city. Only one conversation was productive and that might not be the right word to describe it. I spoke to one of the officers of the SNL homeowners association." He raised his hands in front of the screen. "It's not Saturday Night Live. It's the Slaters and Neighboring Lanes townhome association or something like that. She's the neighborhood busybody. She said she might have seen Tricia Barton, Jane's mother, at Jane's home on the day of the assault."

"Wow!" said Lin.

"She also dropped over to Jane's place earlier in the day herself," McCarthy added. "She brought a plant with her. It was a subterfuge. She apparently just wanted an excuse to look around."

"That explains the plant," Stone said, looking at Katz, who recalled seeing it on the kitchen counter on Sunday night. "What was this woman's name?" Stone asked.

"Jenkins or Judkins, something like that. I have it written down somewhere. I'll find it during our meeting or else I'll email it to you

111

afterwards."

"We need to talk to Tricia Barton," said Katz.

"How do you want to handle it, Sherry?" asked McCarthy. "Do you want to contact Barton yourself? Do you want us to do it? Should we do it together?"

"I've tried to reach her a couple of times," Stone said. "David has been reaching out to her as well. She's pretty much incommunicado. I'm beginning to wonder if she's avoiding us, to be honest. If she is deliberately avoiding us, it raises a suspicion that she was involved in the assault. I'm going to give it a couple more days. Then I'm going to drive over to her house and talk to her."

"Have you ever met her?" asked Katz. Stone said she had not. "Well, you're in for a real shock," he said. "She looks just like Jane. Be prepared. When you see her, your first thought is that Jane's been released from the hospital and is recuperating at her mother's place. The resemblance is uncanny."

"It's freaky," said Santana. "I remember seeing them together at the reception at the Principle Gallery when Jane first joined our office."

As the conversation proceeded, Stone conducted a word search of the SNL Homeowners Association. McCarthy must have known the woman's name, she thought. It was silly for him to be hiding information. She understood they were all holding their cards close; she was probably the worst offender in that regard. It took her about ten minutes to find Kyle Judkis. Then she texted Reese. She asked whether he had interviewed her. He said no. She texted back: "Get in touch with her immediately. No need to mention Mac. Ask her about her Jane. Pretend as though you don't know anything about her. See if she tells you about the plant. I'm primarily interested about her seeing Jane's mother at the house. Feel her out. Find out as much as you can and relay the information to me. Thanks."

The others could see Stone texting on her phone. Lin suspected she was communicating with Reese, who was seated beside her. She figured it had something to do with the secret Stone had previously shared with him, the one that kept him up at night. Lin concluded that Stone was triangulating people on the call. Stone suspected McCarthy, Santana, or Katz of doing something, Lin concluded. She believed she was in the clear, or else Stone would not have divulged anything to Reese.

After Reese stopped texting, Lin handed the baby to him and he went off to put the baby in his crib. While he was gone, she turned off the video camera, picked up his phone, and scrolled through his messages. By the time he returned, she had put down the phone and turned on the video. The others had seen the screen go black in Reese's absence.

"Anything else?" Katz asked McCarthy.

"Nothing comes to mind," he said.

Santana and Lin then briefed the group about Suzanne Marconi and the phone message to Hutton about Hank Simon.

"It turns out they serve on the BOM Board of Directors together," Lin said. "I didn't find anything controversial, however, either about Mr. Simon or his fiber optic company, GlassGrass. He scrupulously avoids anything that could be personally or professionally embarrassing. As soon as an issue arises, he has an army of people who go online and make the controversy disappear. It almost looks as though these people live online to put out online fires."

"Sorry to interrupt," McCarthy said. "I just got an email from one of our criminal attorneys about a fraud task force report. Mai, can you send it to him right away? He claims it's urgent."

"I'm on it," she said. "I'm stepping away for a quick minute. I'll be back as soon as I get this taken care of." They did that all the time, picking up other office tasks while working on Hutton's case.

"Let's listen to the message," Katz said.

McCarthy raised his phone to the microphone on his computer. He pressed a button on the phone and the message played:

"Jane, this is Suzanne Marconi. This is uncomfortable. One of my employees in Richmond is leveling allegations, threatening to file a complaint of some sort. I've been told it could be sent to your office. If it does, please don't take any precipitous action. The allegations are spurious. Now I don't expect you to take my word for it. I know you hate Simon. Plus there's no love lost between you and me. But please don't take what she says at face value, despite how things ended up between the two of you. Any action on your part is retaliation, as far as I'm concerned. If you want war, you'll get it. Both inside and outside of the courtroom. People die on the battlefield; bodies are carried off on stretchers. I'm not threatening you but I'll do everything in my power to make sure you rue the day."

McCarthy leaned back in his chair, entwined his fingers and cupped them behind his head. "I've listened to this recording about a dozen times. The more I listen to it, the more convinced I am that it doesn't have anything to do with Hank Simon at all. I think there are two separate messages being conveyed."

"Go on," Katz said.

"The first message is that there's a complaint. The second is that there is discord between Jane, on the one hand, and Simon and Marconi on the other hand. I think Marconi was telling Jane that any action on her part would be interpreted as some kind of vendetta against her and Simon. She was claiming foul play."

"What foul play?" asked Katz.

A momentary silence followed. Then Santana said: "I just did a search on Hank Simon. He was romantically involved with Tricia Barton."

"Jane Hutton's mother?" Lin asked excitedly. She had just rejoined the conversation.

A phone rang. Everyone glanced at their phones. Katz picked up his.

The others watched and listened. "Yeah, this is Mo Katz," he said. "That's right." More listening. "Good to hear from you. How's Jane doing?" Lin, McCarthy, and Santana watched as Katz turned his face away from the camera. They could only see the left side of his face. "When did this happen?" he asked. More listening. "Well, first of all, thanks for thinking to call me." He reached over and muted his microphone. He stood and walked away from the computer, out of view.

"What's going on?" asked McCarthy.

"It's obviously from the hospital," Lin said. "It must be a status on Jane. I hope she's still alive."

None of them spoke. The only sound was the classical music playing in the background on someone's stereo. "What's that music?" Santana asked to fill the void. Then he answered his own question. "I recognize it," Santana said. "It's the soundtrack from *Ocean's 11*." A minute later, Lin sent everyone the link to the movie's scene outside the Bellagio where Claude Debussy's *Clair de Lune* played as the actors watched the fountain waters dance.

Katz returned and unmuted his computer. "We've got a situation," he said. "I just got a call from a guard at Johns Hopkins."

"Is Jane okay?" asked Lin.

"Yes," Katz said. "Sorry, everyone. Jane is fine. This was not about her. It was about someone who turned up at her hospital room. As I was saying, one of the guards called me about a woman with an official ID. A nurse said she found the woman trying to manipulate the tubes and machines that are keeping Jane alive."

"You mean someone tried to kill her?" Lin was alarmed.

"Maybe," Katz said, putting out his hand in front of the screen as though he was a cop stopping traffic at an intersection. "Let's not rush to any conclusions." The phone rang again. "Hold on," he said. He muted the microphone again.

"This is crazy," said McCarthy. "He can't exclude us from these conversations. We're a team. We have a right to know what the hell is going on."

Although they could not hear Katz, he could hear them. He unmuted the microphone even though he was still on the phone.

He turned on the speaker. The others heard the remainder of the conversation: "…tracking her phone. It's on the Baltimore Washington Parkway returning to D.C. So it's her, or at least someone in possession of her phone. What do you want us to do?"

"Nothing right now," Katz said. "I simply wanted confirmation. I'm going to call her now. If I'm not satisfied with her explanation, I'll call you back." He hung up the phone and looked into the camera on his computer. "Sorry," he said. "I didn't mean to exclude you. Mac's right. We're a team. For a minute, I wasn't sure what I was dealing with. I thought Jane might be dead and I did not want that news communicated to you by a third party."

"What's up, boss?" asked Santana.

"That was PerSec," he said, referring to the personnel security office. "I asked them to check on the whereabouts of Sally Orr's phone."

"Orr?" McCarthy asked, astonished.

"Sally is the one who went to Baltimore and used her ID to gain access to Jane's room," Katz explained. "I wasn't sure if it was her, or someone with her ID, but the guard described her accurately and PerSec reports her phone is currently somewhere on the B.W. Parkway. I'm confident now that it's her."

"What the fuck," Santana uttered. Katz shared his confusion and exasperation. They had been in the middle of a discussion about Barton. They seemed to be making progress. Maybe they were close to a breakthrough; it surely felt that way to Katz. Now the focus had shifted to one of their own. "I guess I shouldn't be entirely surprised," Santana said. "Sally's name keeps popping up in our conversations."

Katz was already phoning her. He had the call on the speaker.

"Sally Orr."

"Sally, it's Mo. Where are you? What's going on?"

"I'm heading back from the hospital. I went to see Jane. She's not doing well. I tried to adjust her pillows and I think one of the nurses thought I was messing around with the equipment at her bedside.

It's okay. I got everything worked out. But she's not in a good place, Mo. I think she's basically on life support now." Orr started to cry. "It's so sad. Everything is sad. There are bodies in Baltimore. There are bodies everywhere. This is out of control."

Katz did not tell her that he had the conversation on the speaker. He studied the expression on Lin's face. McCarthy was away from his computer and the screen showed an empty chair. Santana had turned off his camera. "Why didn't you tell me that you were going up there?" Katz asked.

"I did. I sent you an email yesterday about five in the afternoon. I never heard back from you. I figured it was okay for me to go."

Katz scanned the dozens of emails in his account. He found it. She had sent it at 5:15 p.m. The email read: "I am planning to visit Jane Hutton tomorrow. Let me know if it's a problem. If I don't hear back from you, I'll assume it's okay to go. Thanks." He shook his head. "I see it," he said. "Thanks."

"Why? Did something happen?"

"One of the security guards thought the worst," Katz said. "She obviously overreacted. It's all good. Thanks. Have a safe drive home." He felt bad about the situation and added, "This is a tough time for all of us. People have friends and family who are affected, physically and financially. We'll get through this, Sally. And we have to hold out hope for Jane."

The call ended.

"Listen," Katz said to the team, still on the computer screen. "Let's recess. I need to decompress. We'll resume at the top of the hour. Everyone hang in there." Without protest, they disconnected. As they did so, a series of beeps and bleeps emitted from their computers. Stone thanked everyone for their work. She indicated that neither she nor Reese would participate in the next call. They had other work to do.

Katz put in a call to Santana. "Should we order surveillance on Sally?"

117

Santana was headed outside of Stone's townhouse to have a smoke. "Yes," he said. He lit a cigarette and walked down the sidewalk toward Columbus Street. The street was deserted. There were no pedestrians in sight. All of the vehicles were parked along the curb. No cars were moving along the street. "I think she had motive for being passed up for the position. I also don't completely buy her story about driving up to Baltimore to check on Hutton. Who would do that?" The truth was no one, or so he felt. "I think we watch her online and rummage through her files. There might be something there. If you want, I can do it. Everyone else's plate is pretty full."

After the call ended, Katz went to the kitchen made an espresso. He sat on the patio and drank it. He regretted questioning Orr's motives but felt he had no choice in the matter. Everyone was suspect. He finished his drink and went back inside.

"Where were we?" he asked the group as they came back online.

"I was explaining that Hank Simon and Tricia Barton were romantically involved," Santana said. "I sent everyone the link about 10 minutes ago." The others scanned their emails and opened the link. The article read:

The Street.
Word on The Street is that Tricia Barton and Hank Simon are a dish.
They were spotted at Anafre DC.
They were enjoying Vuelve a la vida Ceviche.
Translated, "Coming back to life." 'Nuf said.
The Street wonders if they peel and devein more than shrimp.

Accompanying the article was a photo of a couple. The man looked like John Houston in *Chinatown*; the woman resembled Jane Hutton.

"This is interesting," Katz said. "Where does it leave us?"

"Pretty much where we started," McCarthy said. "We need to interview Barton. I think Marconi and Simon are a diversion, but we can pursue that angle if you think it's worth it. As to Orr, I'm inclined to believe her story."

"I agree on all counts," Katz said. He did not share his one-off with Santana. He felt it was poor form to question the integrity of someone in the office and wanted to keep that inquiry between himself and Santana. "Marconi and Simon may be important, but the primary focus has to be on Tricia Barton. Her name starts to appear everywhere we look."

*

LIN CALLED CRAIG. "Sorry to bother you," she said. "But I wonder if you can shed any light on Ms. Marconi's relationship with Hank Simon. He's a new member of the BOM Board of Directors."

"No bother," said Craig. "It's good to hear from you."

"What can you tell me about Mr. Simon?"

"I can tell you that Hank Simon is filthy rich, as in he's one of the richest people on the face of the earth. But he's also clean as a whistle. There's never been even a whiff of impropriety about him."

"How do you know?"

"He was vetted before he was named to the board. The information was privileged and confidential but I got to look at some of it as Ms. Marconi's executive assistant. The guy is apparently a ruthless businessman but he's a straight shooter and has never been accused of anything fraudulent, which is pretty amazing when you consider he built an empire out of a tiny fiber optics company based in Northern Virginia."

"Hmm," she said. She was disappointed. Lin was ready to say goodbye.

"The person I think you should be looking at is his nephew, David Simon," Craig said. "He's the black sheep of the family. If anyone's been involved in any shady dealings, it's him."

119

"David Simon?" asked Lin. That name had never come up. She jotted it down on a piece of paper. "Hmm, good to know. Can I play a tape for you?" she asked. She opened the link on an email and played the recording of Marconi's message that McCarthy had shared that morning.

"Do you have any idea what she's talking about?" Lin asked. As she posed the question, she knew she was breaking protocol. Katz would be livid if he knew what she was doing. No one had authorized her to pursue leads pertaining to Marconi and Simon. In fact, Tricia Barton was now the primary person of interest. Furthermore, she was providing potential evidence to an individual who might be a suspect in the case. Just as Sally Orr appeared on the team's radar, it was possible that Craig was implicated in the assault.

"Yes," he said. "David Simon has a stable of companies that receive government contracts to provide services at public housing facilities in New Jersey," he explained. "The services are performed by subcontractors. There's nothing illegal in what he's doing, *per se*."

"You're suggesting something unethical, Craig," she said.

"So now I'm going off the record," he said. "I wouldn't normally do this, Mai. But there was something about our previous conversation. We connected. I can read people, maybe because I don't see too well. And I got a very positive vibe from you."

"I got the same," she confided. "You can trust me. I'll preserve your confidentiality, I promise. If you share anything with me that's germane to the investigation, I'll be sure we take appropriate safeguards."

"Fair enough," he said. "Except I'm pretty sure you have the information I'm going to share with you. Jane took it with her. I know because I packaged it up. I was reluctant to tell you about it the last time we spoke."

"Okay."

Craig hesitated. He sighed. Then he said, "On second thought, I'm not going to tell you. You know where to look. You can figure it out for yourself."

"Okay," said Lin. She didn't sound disappointed. She was up for the challenge.

*

"YOU DID WHAT?" Katz was livid.

"I'm sorry, Mo," Lin said. "Curtis said we had to look at it. So I got it. And I struck pay dirt." She had gone to the office and retrieved the thumb drive. She had completed an initial review of the files and found plenty of information about David Simon.

"Okay, go on," he said.

"According to the information in Jane's file," she said, "subcontractors do work for Mr. Simon under federal contracts but don't get paid with the proceeds of those contracts. The subcontractors are paid by other parties for doing the same work. Simon pockets the money he gets from the federal government.

"The scheme is similar to one prosecuted last month in the Eastern District of California. In that case, the defendant had contracts with the Army and Air Force. He used subcontractors to provide goods and services of some sort. Instead of paying the subcontractors, he spent the money at casinos and restaurants. The amount of fraud totaled $3.7 million and the defendant got nearly five years in prison."

"What did the defendant plead to in the California case?"

"One count of mail fraud," Lin said. "I don't have the details and I don't know what was involved in the plea negotiations. If you want, I can call out there and get that information."

"It won't be necessary," Katz said. "It's pretty clear David Simon clearly crossed the line into criminality." He thought for a minute and added, "How much money are we talking about?"

"It's somewhere in the order of $5 million. Based on my math, Simon faced 60 plus months in the penitentiary."

Katz looked at his research assistant on the screen. "This was

121

great work, Mai. I commend you. It's not the first time you've gone outside the lines to track down information. I remember you going to Crystal City when we were tracking down the murderer in the Jones Point case. Good work. Anything else?"

"Yes," she said, beaming. "But it's purely speculative on my part." Katz nodded for her to proceed. "Suppose Marconi is one of Simon's subcontractors?" she asked. "I don't believe Marconi would have contacted Jane unless she knew that a complaint was already in Jane's hands. Otherwise, it would have been a tip-off. Jane wasn't going to do Marconi any favors. The two hate each other. So Marconi learned about it because the whistleblower was one of her employees. She was trying to work herself out of a jam."

Katz did some quick research while Lin spoke. Her image remained in the upper right-hand corner of his computer screen. Then, when he finished and began speaking, both of their images appeared. He watched himself as he spoke, noticing his hair was growing out of the bounds of his normally conservative cut. "I'm on her website now," he said. "She's affiliated with over 20 businesses, half of which she owns. They're in real estate, hospitality, and public housing." He thought to himself that real estate and the hospitality industry were being walloped by the coronavirus. "She has a series of contracts with Simon, a New Jersey-based operation."

"I think we're on to something," she said.

"Maybe, but what?" He studied Marconi's website. "Here's what we have to do, Mai. We need to figure out whether Simon and Marconi put in any bids in connection with COVID-19 contracts. If they sought an award, they might have used the same fraudulent scheme that you mentioned to me."

"I'll get started on the research right away."

*

THERE WAS a tremendous demand for ventilators, protective masks and gloves, hospital beds, and virus tests. Governors demanded more assistance from the federal government. The federal government promised results it could not meet. Private companies redoubled production. Supply chains shifted from the international to the domestic market. States competed against one another. The bureaucratic process was slow and ineffective. And nation states hoarded equipment for their own people as the international marketplace collapsed and nationalistic sentiment affected the supply chain.

As a result, the need to combat COVID-19 spawned a cottage industry in which fraud was rampant. States and federal agencies, anxious to pay any price for the goods and equipment, entered into deals with crooks and shysters who were only too eager to take advantage of their plight. Promises were made for items that could not be delivered. Contracts were signed for goods that did not exist. Phony dates were given to meet unrealistic timetables and dishonest numbers were quoted to produce unattainable volumes of items.

Money exchanged hands without attention to fine print in the contracts. Other contracts were made on the phone or online using signature blocks that could not be traced to real people or real companies. In the mad rush that ensued, mistakes were made at every point in the process. People profited unfairly from the confusion and chaos. A fog of war covered the zone in which doctors, nurses, and first responders sought to stem the tide.

The outflow of federal dollars was unparalleled. Within less than a month, the federal government was expending close to the equivalent of the nation's $4 trillion annual budget.

On top of that, many states were writing checks for goods and services without consulting one another or even using standard operating procedures to coordinate with their own agencies.

It was a field day for people out to make a fast buck.

Lin discovered that charging documents in the COVID-19 case she referenced to Katz had been filed on Friday, the 10th, two days before Hutton was attacked. Lin wondered whether it was possible similar charges were under consideration against Simon and Marconi.

*

THE ENTIRE OFFICE held a virtual happy hour on Saturday. Katz's computer screen was filled with images of smiling colleagues, some dressed in exotic costumes. It was a far cry from the somber faces that greeted the all-hands meeting following Hutton's attack. Today everyone was letting off steam and joining in virtual revelry. Some had missed St. Patrick's Day celebrations and it appeared likely they'd also be missing Cinco de Mayo. Everyone had missed Opening Day. (Everyone wondered when the baseball team would hoist the World Series banner at Nats Park.) Late season skiing trips had been cancelled as well as summer cruises and vacations. They needed *something*.

As Katz watched his staff celebrate, it occurred to him that he had never scheduled an after-hours get-together for his entire staff. In the two-and-a-half years he had held his position, he had joined small groups after work at local restaurants to discuss cases, but never anything like this. Sure, there were celebrations in the main conference room, plenty of them, including a holiday open house when the judges, clerks, and folks from sister agencies dropped over; retirements; showers; and significant milestones, like a 60th birthday party. Katz sponsored a barbecue last summer, which was marred by rain. Yet this was something special, the likes of which they had never experienced before.

Two months ago, if someone had suggested a virtual happy hour, people would have rolled their eyes. No one even used the video conferencing apps. They all talked about how they needed to transition to a virtual workplace, with more teleconferences and teleworking. But that's all it was, talk. No one took it seriously, particularly Katz, who was a bit old school and felt people had to be in the office in order to be productive. Katz believed you needed to sit across the table from other people and look them in the eyes to conduct business.

The past month had radically changed his thinking. He was discovering two things that had eluded him. First, he could actually observe more on the screen than in a room. The mannerisms of every person participating in a conversation were on display. He could watch them without staring or letting on that he was studying their expressions. The second was that he could multitask on a conference call in ways that were unimaginable in a conference room. All of his files were instantly at his disposal. Proof positive was the way the team was uncovering clues in Hutton's case. Lin, Santana, and McCarthy had all jumped online and researched items in real time while the group was discussing the issue.

Snowe came up behind him holding two cups of coffee. "We had one of these events the other night. Who would have thought? This just might be the new normal." She put down a cup. "Maybe you'd prefer a shot of tequila?"

He laughed. "It's pretty cool. And, what's really good about it is no one notices when you leave." Katz was notorious for slipping in and out of meetings and social events.

"You know what else?" She left and then returned with a paper in hand. "You can study people in ways you've never been able to do before. Listen to this interview of Alfred Hitchcock with Pia Lindstrom in 1972 about *Rear Window*. Hitchcock said:

'I had to cut to what he saw, then cut back to his reaction. Now, what I was really doing was showing a mental process of the man by means of pictures, by what he saw.'

"Pretty interesting, huh? That described perfectly how video conferences enable you to study people's reactions in real time. Earlier, I watched the way you looked at the members of your team. You're studying someone's mental process on the basis of their reactions, aren't you?"

"If you're watching me watching them, what do you think I'm

125

doing?"

"You suspect someone on your team of complicity in Jane's attack."

He glanced at her but said nothing.

"I'll let you get back to your party," she said. "Just don't stay too late!"

Some attorneys performed skits. Others played instruments and read passages from their favorite plays, sometimes separately and sometimes in combination with other staff members. People were dressed as historic figures and popular personalities. There was an Egyptian Pharaoh, Marie Antoinette, and Alexander Hamilton. The Blues Brothers appeared on two separate screens, replete with shades and hats, singing "Hold On, I'm Social Distancing." Others created backgrounds to mimic famous paintings. One group dressed as the characters in *Luncheon of the Boating Party* by Renoir. There were featured songs and parodies, including a version of Bob Dylan's *Everyone Must Get Stoned* entitled *Everybody Must Stay Home*. Someone did a rendition of The Rolling Stones' *You Can't Always Get What You Want*. Edgar Allen Poe look-alikes made a couple of appearances. And there was L.B. Jefferies, the convalescing photographer played by Jimmy Stewart in *Rear Window*, dressed in pajamas with his leg in a cast and holding a telescopic lens. Obviously, it was a movie for the times.

The event was billed as happy hour but it quickly morphed into the happy evening. Katz remained online for a couple of hours and made some remarks commending the staff for originality and imagination. People slipped away and returned to the party all evening. Someone mentioned that the "One World: Together At Home" concert was streaming. Someone else posted the email to make donations. Several wrote that it was the best party the office had ever sponsored. One person emailed "We should do it again next year." No one responded to that suggestion. One and done was more like it.

Katz signed off around 9 p.m. He joined Snowe, who was watching an episode of "Grace and Frankie." She said, "I don't know how I missed this show. I thought it was a movie. It's been on for something like six seasons. Both Jane Fonda and Lily Tomlin are fantastic." They stayed up half the night watching Fonda with Lee Marvin in *Cat Ballou* and Lily Tomlin with Art Carney in *The Late Show*. They wandered up to bed bleary-eyed at three in the morning.

Sunday was a sleep-in day, without any rules about maintaining social distance. By the time Snowe and Katz got to their Sunday newspapers and coffee, it was already afternoon. In the evening, he considered the suspects in Hutton's attack. Despite his desire to eliminate Sally Orr as a suspect, he needed confirmation from Johns Hopkins that she was not interfering with efforts to resuscitate Hutton. Marconi and David Simon were more likely suspects, although he needed to acquire a better understanding of their federal contracts before he could make a judgment about either or both of them. Tricia Barton also made an appearance on the list of probable suspects. To date, she had evaded both Stone and members of Katz's team.

*

YET ANOTHER EMAIL. One was enough. Two were incriminating. A third was proof beyond a reasonable doubt. There was no way these emails would be disregarded in a court of law.

"I grow despondent. I now realize how little I meant to you. You have not validated my actions by expressing your love. In fact, my actions have driven you away. Do you recoil at the thought of me? Has my image been tarnished beyond recognition? I am beside myself. I wonder if I am supposed to pray for Jane's recovery. Will it exonerate me? Will she claim she does not remember who attacked her? Is it possible that she will have a memory loss, either real or feigned? If so, will we return to normal? Is there even a normal to which to return? We live in such a torturous time. The

virus is infecting all of us. We all test positive. It seeps under the door like a gas. It penetrates the windows and walls of my home. It fills my clothes. I cannot wash away the stain. I have become the virus. I am the Angel of Death. I am the one who plunged the knife into Jane's abdomen. I alone watched as she bled. I left the house confident she was dying a slow and painful death. I am the disease."

Chapter Three: MARCONI

SUZANNE MARCONI and David Simon walked along the C&O Canal towpath in Georgetown. The walkway cut through the lower half of Georgetown, which had grown up on either side of it like a lush garden on the banks of a stream. There were only a few other pedestrians outdoors.

To avoid detection, it was smarter for them to meet outside than to communicate online. Phone, email, text, and video messages left an electronic footprint. On the other hand, with phones left at home, Marconi and Simon felt safe from discovery. Plus, with masks covering half of their faces, they were unrecognizable in broad daylight.

They walked shoulder to shoulder with their heads bent as if in prayer.

"You really messed this up," Simon said. "First, I told you to give her a piece of the action. It was no loss to you. But no. You refused to follow my advice because you're a greedy …." He stopped himself. There was no need saying things for which he would apologize later. "You wanted it all for yourself," he said.

"Calm down, David," she said. "Show a little bit of that steely resolve your uncle Hank is known for, will you? This is not a problem."

"Don't talk to me about my uncle." He was irritated. "Do you have any idea how long and hard I've worked to get my company in its current position?" He paused. "A decade. And now with things really opening up for me, you make a move that could jeopardize everything."

Under normal circumstances, Simon would be at his company's headquarters in Paterson, New Jersey, celebrating the approval of contracts with the U.S. Department of Housing and Community Development and the Veterans Administration to provide comprehensive cleaning services at federal facilities and housing developments up and down the East Coast.

Simon selected Paterson for strategic reasons. Paterson had a large immigrant population and the highest percentage of individuals with disabilities of any city with more than 100,000 residents. A company headquartered in Paterson was a perfect candidate for federal dollars to provide job opportunities for disadvantaged workers. With the coronavirus causing unemployment to spike to heights similar to those of The Great Depression, the need to assist workers and businesses was greater than ever.

The message was displayed for all to see on a large billboard in the middle of Paterson that read, "Simon Says *Do as I Do*: Lend a Hand!" The billboard showed two hands grasping one another. David Simon, known for hyperbole, said he got the inspiration for the sign from Michelangelo's *The Creation of Adam*.

His latest coup was worth $10 million. It involved leveraging a service that he provided infrequently, namely, cleaning up after unattended deaths or suicides. His employees entered homes and businesses wearing extensive protective garb to clean and disinfect surfaces with elaborate cleaning solutions and make the grotesque death disappear. Today that service was in high demand with every business exposed to COVID-19, including office buildings, restaurants, and retail stores.

Simon used Marconi's subcontractors to staff his contracts while Marconi turned to public and private vendors to fund the same job at the same time. In some instances, the work was billed three times, resulting in payments from federal and municipal governments as well as private companies. So long as the double or triple billing was not too obvious, it slipped under the radar. Or at least it did until the whistleblower came along.

When one of Marconi's managers got wise to their operation and asked for a piece of the action a few months ago, Simon told Marconi to give her some money to keep her mouth shut. Marconi said it would set the wrong precedent. *Who gives a fuck about precedent?* Simon thought to himself. Marconi refused the request. After being rebuffed, the manager called a hotline for complaints about waste, fraud and abuse. Somehow, she got connected to Jane Hutton in the U.S. Attorney's office in the Eastern District of Virginia. Hutton reached out to the woman, who claimed to possess two sets of books, including one that cooked the numbers.

The complaint came at the worst possible time. Given the demand to combat COVID-19, Simon's business was thriving.

"I never expected you to reach out to that attorney, Hutton," he said. "I was just sharing the information. If you were going to take the next step, you should have consulted me." He lowered his mask. "It's only a matter of time before someone finds your phone message. When they do, everything we've put together the past several years is at risk."

Frustration built inside of him. He had spent years amassing millions in federal government contracts. He had cautiously created an enterprise the likes of which had not been seen since the days of Bernie Madoff. Simon even paid off a congressional aide to pressure a federal contract office to grant him contracts as seed money back in 2014.

He had particular reason for concern given the current environment. The public was incensed at any profiteering during the coronavirus crisis. The story about an entrepreneur in Tennessee who had stockpiled nearly 18,000 bottles of hand sanitizer to sell at exorbitant prices was widely circulated. The guy was simply operating under the law of supply and demand, Simon thought, and far as he could tell, wasn't even doing anything illegal. Yet the public outrage was so great that he ended up donating his supplies to people in need and the Tennessee attorney general's office was breathing down his neck and conducting an investigation into price gouging.

Then there was that case in Maryland, where the state was cancelling a $12 million overdue order for ventilators and protective masks from a political fundraiser. The Maryland attorney general's office had received a referral about the matter.

The Federal Emergency Management Agency was getting ready to cancel a $55.5 million no-bid contract for respiratory masks with a company after it discovered the company had no experience in producing masks and its parent company was in bankruptcy.

Everywhere he looked, public companies like Shake Shack, Ruth's Chris Steak House, and even the Los Angeles Lakers basketball team were returning federal monies received under aid packages passed by Congress.

None of them broke the law. Public perception damned them. Anyone believed to be taking advantage of the COVID-19 crisis was under indictment. Imagine if a legitimate whistleblower complaint was lodged against a company? It made Simon sick just to think of it. If the complaint against him was thoroughly investigated, he would face financial ruin, his reputation would be shot, and he stood a good chance of going to jail.

"I mean, really, how could you be so stupid?" he asked, the frustration boiling over. "You know you're never supposed to leave a message for someone on the phone. If they don't answer, you just hang up. If you have to leave a message, you say something innocuous like, 'Call me back when you have a minute.' You don't make threats on the line. That's what you did and now she's dead." He pushed his mask over the bridge of his nose and adjusted the elastic straps around his ears.

"First, I don't need a lecture from you," Marconi said. "Second, you wouldn't be living the high life if it wasn't for me. I set up the subcontractors and I've basically run your operation for years. Third, I did not threaten her. And, fourth, Hutton is not dead, so quit saying that." She looked at him. With her nose and mouth covered by a mask, her eyes were all he saw, and those eyes were large and menacing. "If I had known any of this was going to happen, I never would have left that message. I regret it. But how did I know that someone was going to attack her?"

He glared back. "I'm only going to ask you this one time," he said. "Was it you? Are you the one who whacked her?"

Now she pulled down her mask. She shouted every expletive that existed in the English language. It continued for several minutes. When she finished, she took a deep breath and concluded, "I can't believe you're asking me that question. Are you out of your mind? Maybe I should be the one asking you: Did you try to kill Jane Hutton?"

"Lower your voice, Suzanne," he instructed.

"I'm not going to be quiet," she continued to scream. "You've got a lot of nerve accusing me of hurting her." A repetition of the invective ensued. In conclusion, she said, "You should be thanking me. I only ever contacted her to drive her away from you."

"Thank you," he said sarcastically. "Thank you very much. When we're both sitting in the federal penitentiary, I'll be singing your praises."

Thirty minutes later, Marconi sat in her car, unnerved. Would anyone find the recording? If someone found it, would they connect it to the file? And if they did both those things, would they investigate her and Simon's fraudulent activities? It seemed unlikely.

She also thought about the circumstances that led her to call Hutton. Simon told her that Hutton had received a whistleblower complaint about him. It was true he did not specifically ask her to call Hutton, but he had insinuated as much, hadn't he? She asked herself how Simon could have thought otherwise. The women knew one another. Hutton had been counsel for BOM and Marconi was the chairman of the board. They parted on less than friendly terms. Marconi thought Hutton acted behind her back by forging an agreement with the U.S. Attorney without first consulting her.

Marconi had two questions. The first was how Simon knew about the whistleblower complaint. Who told him? The most likely suspect was Hutton's mother, Tricia Barton. But that implied Hutton shared private business with her mother, which seemed unlikely.

The second question was whether Simon attacked Hutton. It

seemed improbable, but it was not out of the question, Marconi concluded. Simon had too much to lose if an inquiry was launched. And COVID-19 provided the perfect smokescreen for him to attempt a serious crime. The likelihood of witnesses seeing him arrive at or leave her house was remote, and the prospect of a thorough police investigation was compromised by the diversion of people and resources due to the coronavirus.

Marconi pushed the ignition and headed home to Foxhall Road, wondering if she had just interacted with the murderer.

As Marconi headed home, Simon continued walking along the towpath. He wondered about the warning he received last week about the whistleblower's complaint. Was it possible that his source had attacked her? He hoped not. It was better to spend a few months in jail for a white-collar crime than a lifetime in prison for murder.

Part Three

The Rundown
Monday, April 20, to Friday, April 24

Evil propels me, and reform of evil propels me .... I stand indifferent,
My gait is no faultfinder's or rejecter's gait,
I moisten the roots of all that has grown.

– Walt Whitman, *Leaves of Grass* (22) 470-472

Chapter One: SIMON

THE CORONAVIRUS task force was holding a press conference when Katz turned on the television. To date, 755,533 cases were reported in the U.S., with 41,379 deaths. Worldwide, 2.39 million people were infected and 165,636 had died. In one week, domestic job growth from the past ten years had evaporated; jobless claims topped 22 million. There was carnage wherever one looked.

Snowe was sitting next to Katz in the living room reading *The New York Times* on her tablet. He asked her, "What was it Ezra Pound said about April? 'April is the cruelest month'?"

"It was T.S. Eliot, not Pound." she replied. "It's from *The Wasteland*." She hit some keys on the tablet, found the poem, and recited:

'April is the cruelest month, breeding

Lilacs out of the dead land, mixing

Memory and desire, stirring

Dull roots with spring rain.'

As she read from the poem, Katz picked up his own tablet and began running through emails. One message was from Shorter, the IT guy, who wrote: "You're in luck. I've got copies of a couple of the conversations. I'm downloading the links now and will email them to you as soon as I'm finished. Stay well! D"

Katz concluded that "stay well" was now a standard farewell, like "have a nice day" or "have a good one." It was no longer about having a good time. It was about survival.

Katz emailed his gratitude and asked how many conversations existed on tape. The response came back a few seconds later: "Four. March 11, 13, 16 and 18. Then you switched to another platform, the one you're currently using. None of those are preserved. Call if you need details. D"

The important thing to Katz was that at least some of the conversations were preserved. He would be able to study Hutton and her surrounding environment. In all likelihood, there was not going to be anything of value. Still, it was worth a look.

The videos were emailed an hour later. Each video consisted of a conversation between Katz, Santana, McCarthy, Hutton, Lin, Orr, and two other senior attorneys. This was the group he assembled three times a week after teleworking was initiated on a voluntary basis. Several of the participants remained in their offices until late March or early April, when mandatory teleworking was imposed.

His only interest was in Jane Hutton.

The tape of Wednesday, March 11, showed her in her office. On the wall was a copy of her law degree from Catholic University and certificates of admission into the Virginia and D.C. bars. On the cabinet behind her were two photos. One showed two women who looked like twins: Hutton and her mother, Tricia Barton. The other photo showed Hutton standing beside a mountain bike dressed in cycling garb. The background suggested it was taken along the Blue Ridge Parkway.

In the tapes for Friday, March 13, and Monday, March 16, Hutton was again at her office desk. The background was identical to the first teleconference call. There were no papers or files in the video.

The fourth and final teleconference was Wednesday, March 18. It showed Hutton in her kitchen. She wore glasses, which reflected light from the screen in front of her. That was the first time Katz had seen her in glasses. He assumed she wore contacts to the office and had switched to old reading glasses. Her hair was pulled back into a knot at the back of her neck, but messy wisps hung down around her face. She was wearing a sweatshirt from her undergraduate alma mater, Holy Cross.

Directly behind her was the kitchen stove with the stainless steel exhaust hood overhead. The hood was like an aluminum hat on her head, giving her a Tin Man look. There were counters on either side of her. Katz carefully reviewed the items on the counters.

On one side was a large vase containing mixing spoons; a set of salt and pepper shakers; a cheese grater in the shape of the Eiffel Tower; and a digital assistant speaker. On the other side was a pewter cup, a coffee maker, an espresso machine, a coffee bean grinder, a pepper grinder, a set of cutlery, and a toaster. There was a check or paper stub sticking out from the top of the cup.

Katz tried to manipulate the picture to increase its size but couldn't do it. He emailed Shorter. "I need a close-up of the items on the kitchen counters in the March 18 video. How soon can you get them to me?"

The response was nearly instantaneous. "Ten minutes." It was like ordering carry-out.

*

THE TEAM reassembled for an update. At times, it seemed as though they were going around in circles. Progress had not been as swift as they might have expected, or hoped. Daydreaming during the discussion was not going to help matters. Yet Katz couldn't help it. It was what he did. He tended to go into trances, concocting scenes in his mind. At times they felt real and he had difficulty separating reality from dreams.

"*Does the defense rest?*"

"*No, your honor. The defense calls the defendant to the stand.*"

Slowly, the defendant rose and approached the bench. The judge administered the oath and the defendant sat in the witness box.

"*Where were you in the early evening hours of Sunday, April 12th?*"

"*I visited the home of Jane Hutton. My sole purpose was to kill her. I attempted to carry out my plan as soon as I stepped across the threshold of her home. My only regret is that I did not succeed.*"

"*Did you act alone?*"

"*No, I acted in concert with that person!*" *The defendant extended a hand and pointed to an observer seated in the courtroom. Everyone turned and gasped.* "I was compelled to act on that person's behalf. I may have been the one who plunged the knife into Jane Hutton's stomach, but the party who was responsible for my actions is seated over there."

Deputies ran to the aisles and pulled the person from the bench, then hustled the accused to the front of the courtroom. "You sat silently while the defendant stood trial for your misdeeds," the judge said, standing with a black shroud over her head. "You are hereby sentenced to the gallows. At noon on Monday, May 4, you will be taken to the Farmer's Market and strung from the highest tree to wave in the wind until you are dead."

The daydream ended.

Tuning back in, Katz asked, "Do you think the country is going to be opened by May 4?"

"We need more testing," Stone said. "We haven't flattened the curve. We have to put people ahead of business. Of course, we also have to balance the medical needs against the societal needs. If people are well but the economy is ailing, we all suffer." She sounded like a coronavirus task force member.

"All right," Katz said, "any additional progress to report?"

McCarthy went first. "I am continuing to speak to members of SNL and others in the neighborhood. No good leads. Most people were just hunkered down. No one was out. No one knew anything was happening until the sirens sounded and the helicopter landed. As far as enemies, there aren't any. Jane Hutton's life consisted of meeting with her mother, riding her bike, and work. There isn't much else there." He hesitated. "Oh, Sherry, I still have to get that name for you."

"Don't bother," Stone said. "I'm focused on other things. I'm anxious to speak with Tricia Barton. Has anyone been able to get in touch with her?" No one responded. "I'm going to go over to her place later today or tomorrow. It's evident that she's avoiding us. I think she may have information to share. Mo, you're welcome to come along if you'd like."

"Count me in," Katz said. Then he went to the next person. "David?"

Reese shared his screen with Lin. "I've been doing a virtual search of the area around Slaters Lane. Nothing has turned up. Like Sherry said, we're anxious to speak with Hutton's mother."

"Oh," Stone interjected. "We looked into your attorney, Orr, who drove up to Baltimore the other day. Her story checks. She didn't do any funny stuff. The security cop overreacted. She was overzealous, to put it politely. I spoke to her on the phone. She's a little off. I'm not sure what rent-a-cop program she attended to get her badge, but they must have been handing out diplomas if you were willing to pay their fees."

"Fair enough," Katz said. "I never believed Sally would hurt Jane, but it's important that we've eliminated her as a suspect."

"Oh, and by the way, the security guard said she's related to an old client of yours," Stone added.

"That reminds me," Lin said. "The guy who's helping me at Stephens Babcock is Blair Craig. He told me to say 'hi' and 'thank you' to you, Mo. Apparently you cut him a break when you were a city prosecutor in Alexandria."

Katz smiled.

"These people are everywhere," Stone said. "Miscreants whose lives were salvaged from ruin by the compassionate Mo Katz."

"Do I detect a bit of sarcasm?" Katz asked.

"No," she said. "I just don't know why you do it. I say fuck 'em. I don't think it makes any difference in the end. What will be, will be."

Katz strongly disagreed with her statement but said nothing. He believed the criminal justice system could make a difference in a person's life. If you could identify the source of anger or alienation inside a first-time offender, you could offer help that reduced the likelihood of recidivism. Katz subscribed to that philosophy, both as a prosecutor and a defense attorney; it was in his DNA. Time and again, he saw the positive outcomes that resulted from his efforts on behalf of people who were caught in the net of the criminal justice system.

Katz asked Lin if she had any additional information.

"Curtis and I are still looking into the relationship between Suzanne Marconi and David Simon," she said.

"Who?" asked McCarthy.

Lin explained that they had concluded Marconi did not call Hutton about Hank Simon. Rather, Marconi was calling about his nephew, David Simon. Marconi and David Simon were business partners; Marconi supplied subcontracts for work that Simon received from federal and municipal governments, and private companies. In the past, David Simon had been charged with fraud in connection with some of those contracts. Stephens Babcock successfully defended Simon against those charges. For reasons nobody understood, Hutton had files about those cases in her computer. Finally, the complaint that Marconi referenced in her phone message to Hutton was nowhere to be found.

"I can't hear you," McCarthy said to Lin. "You must have put your microphone on mute." He pointed his fingers to his ears.

Lin fiddled with the buttons on her computer screen. "Can you hear me now?" she asked.

"Yes," Katz answered. "What did you say?"

"I was saying that we think Marconi was talking about David Simon and not Hank Simon, who happens to be David's uncle," Lin said. "I'm not sure how we got started down the wrong path, but we have it straightened out now."

Katz looked at everyone's expression. He detected frustration and fatigue, particularly on the faces of McCarthy and Santana. "Okay," he said. "Everyone keep working this case. I'd love to wrap it up in a big bow and present it to Sherry by the end of the week. If we can't find the assailant, the investigation will migrate to the Alexandria Police Department."

As Katz spoke, Lin emailed Marconi to set up an interview.

Santana was on the cc line.

*

"PICK UP!" Marconi bellowed into the phone. As if on cue, Craig answered. "What is this, Blair? I just got an email from someone at the U.S. Attorney's office wanting to speak to me about Jane Hutton. What did you tell them?"

She waited ten seconds and, when Craig did not speak, she continued, "Here is what I am going to tell them. I did not like the legal representation that we received from Hutton in the BOM case. I recommended we fight the criminal charge, but she had no stomach for a fight. She simply did not consult us."

Marconi had no intention of mentioning the phone message to Lin. Instead, she would focus on her relationship with Hutton. She was not certain the U.S. Attorney's office had listened to the recording. If the issue was raised, she would request to consult an attorney before providing any more information.

"Yes, I think I might have called her," she would say. *"I don't remember. Am I suspected of something? Even if I'm not, I think I need to consult an attorney. You never know how an inadvertent comment might be twisted and interpreted as a lie. And I don't want to be accused of anything. I'm trying very hard to be totally honest with you."*

Marconi continued, "Hutton manipulated the Bank of Magellan every step of the way. She wanted us to bleed. In her heart, she was never a defense attorney. I think she was hired by the U.S. Attorney, Mo Katz, because he saw her for who she really is, a Ralph Nader type." Then she pivoted. "So what did you tell that woman in the prosecutor's office?"

"What woman?"

"Don't play dumb with me, Blair. I can see right through your bullshit. You spoke to a woman by the name of Lin. I knew it as soon as she called. What did you tell her?"

"I'm not going to lie," he said. "I spoke with her. I said you were the first person she should contact if she wanted to learn about Jane Hutton's relationship with the bank. I figured that's what you would want me to say. It allows you to shape the narrative."

She doubted Craig was being honest. He was playing to her vanity. She was reasonably certain he had thrown her under the bus. But he had a point. It made sense to start at the top. That's precisely what she would have told him to do. She brushed a hand through her hair. Her nails rain down her scalp like the bristles of a steel comb. Craig always had an explanation and an excuse. "Why is this woman from the prosecutor's office interested in me at all?"

"She's looking for people who might have had a motive to attack Ms. Hutton," Craig said. "It's that simple. We were Hutton's major client. It was complex litigation. People can differ on whether or not they think she did us a favor by settling the case."

"Don't defend Jane," Marconi said. "She was a manipulative bitch. I'm not afraid to tell that to the U.S. Attorney. I don't know who attacked her, and I know I didn't do it, but I wasn't surprised it happened. She enraged people. You know that. You worked with her. She manipulated everybody from every angle. She was poisonous."

Marconi thought of something. "You were demoted at the firm, weren't you? Before she left. She was dissatisfied with your performance. Despite your disability, she felt you weren't handling the case adequately. Maybe you held a grudge? Maybe you're a suspect?"

"I've since been restored to my former position," he said.

Marconi laughed. "But you sued, didn't you? You claimed discrimination."

"I don't know what you're talking about," he replied.

"I think you do, Blair. I think it's only a matter of time before they circle back and question you. I'm sure you've done a good job of throwing them off the trail so far. That woman Lin is probably just some flunky in Katz's office. Just wait until they sic the dogs on you. They'll turn you into a bowl of chop suey."

Marconi was having fun now. Although she doubted Blair might really have had something to do with Hutton's attack, she thought of him as a Norman Bates type, always a little creepy. The way he looked when he wasn't wearing sunglasses freaked her out. "You better check your calendar as to your whereabouts on the afternoon of April 12th," she said as she ended the call.

*

"MR. KATZ? My name is Ryan Long. I'm with the DOJ Inspector General's Office. Do you have a minute?" The voice was calm, not at all threatening. Yet it sent a chill through Katz. Nobody wanted to hear from the IG. Katz had deleted the email from Long and put it out of his mind. *Out of sight, out of mind.* He held the phone in his hand, hesitating. He knew Long was going to ask for an explanation as to why Katz was devoting time and resources to the Hutton investigation. He hoped there wasn't going to be an effort to shut down the team's work. They might be floundering now, but give it a few more days and they'd turn up something. They had to. There wasn't any alternative, Katz believed. Sherry Stone didn't have the resources to do the job. And if his team was forced to disband, any leads they were developing would be lost.

"How can I help you, Ryan? Do you mind if I call you Ryan?"

"We've had complaints about the amount of time and resources that your office is expending on an investigation that falls under the aegis of the Alexandria Police Department. And I prefer to be called Mr. Long."

The use of the word "aegis" told Katz what to expect. Long was going to be boring, pompous, and difficult. And that was before Long said he preferred to be called by his last name. Katz knew there was nothing to be gained by reacting in a negative manner. It was better to swallow hard and listen.

"Okay, thanks Mr. Long. What can you tell me about these complaints?"

"They have come from unnamed individuals in your office as well as officials from the police department," Long said. "The internal complaint suggests that other important work is falling by the wayside. The outside complaint has to do with your office violating the city's protocols for investigating a crime. I wonder if I could drop by your office and discuss the situation with you?"

If Katz heard right, there were complaints coming from two directions. He had an idea as to the source in his office. But the city? Why would anyone be annoyed that he was trying to assist the police department? Was it possible, he wondered, that Stone felt he was trodding on her turf? He already had a premonition that she and Reese were working their own side investigation and withholding information from him.

"I'm available next week," he said. He knew instinctively that he had jumped and, in so doing, given away the fact that he needed a week to develop a plan.

"I'm sorry, Mr. Katz," Long said. "But this really can't wait until next week. Could I come to your office tomorrow?"

Katz pivoted quickly. "That would be fine," Katz said. "Or even later today."

"Today?" Now Long had spoken too fast.

"Sure, why not? I can accommodate your schedule. What's the earliest time you're available?" Katz chuckled to himself. If he played his cards right, he might actually get a week's time after all.

"What about Thursday?"

"Thursday, the 23rd works for me. How about 4 p.m.?"

"That would be perfectly fine," Long replied. "In preparation for our meeting, I'd appreciate it if you can provide at that time the names of every individual in your office who has worked on the case concerning your former deputy U.S. Attorney; the number of hours each individual spent investigating the matter since Monday, April 13th; the issues that each individual covered; a list of every person they interviewed; and copies of any and all documents assembled in connection with the investigation."

Katz could not abide such instructions. "Do you think the investigation might be jeopardized by providing you with that information while the investigation is ongoing?" he asked.

"If anyone has jeopardized the investigation, sir, sadly it is you."

"I'm sorry?"

"You heard me, Mr. Katz. The U.S. government has devoted nearly $3 trillion to fight the coronavirus. Do you know what that means? It means that every thief, hustler, grifter, felon, hacker, and shyster on the planet is going to try to get their hands on some of that loot. Now, more than any other time in our nation's history, we must be vigilant custodians of the public trust. We have to inspect, prosecute, and oversee the expenditure of that money.

"While we are busy doing our job, you are diverting valuable resources in your office to conduct a police investigation. A police investigation! You are not Sherlock Holmes, Mr. Katz. You are a federal prosecutor. Perhaps it's time you acted like one and joined forces with the rest of us instead of running your own rogue operation."

Katz lost it. "Jane Hutton is the deputy of my civil division," he shot back. "The police department's resources are stretched thin as the city responds to the coronavirus. I'm going to do everything in my God-given power to assist in the search of the person or persons responsible for hurting her."

"It's not your God-given power, Mr. Katz. It's the powers given to you by the United States of America. And, in the opinion of the Inspector General's Office, we think you've gone rogue, to put it bluntly. You are not supposed to be using federal employees to conduct a city investigation. Your actions are as culpable as those of the individuals who are being investigated for fraudulent dealings in connection with COVID-19."

"You've got a lot of nerve saying that, Ryan."

"Thursday at 4 p.m. it is," Long concluded. "I'll see you then.

Please have the materials I've requested at my disposal at that time if you are unable to send them beforehand. And my name is Mr. Long. Good day."

*

KATZ WAS still steaming about his conversation with Long when the phone rang. Katz answered the call on the computer screen and Reese's face popped up. "Did you read the decision?" he asked. Without waiting for an answer, Reese continued, "I didn't even know a jury could read a conviction without it being unanimous."

Reese's final semester in law school was in tatters, his graduation uncertain, and the scheduling of the bar exam up in the air. But that had not dampened his enthusiasm to cover the U.S. Supreme Court's rulings, including the 6-3 decision announced today overturning laws in Louisiana and Oregon and requiring that jury decisions needed to be unanimous to convict defendants of serious crimes. Reese recited from the decision by Justice Neil Gorsuch:

"Whenever we might look to determine what the term 'trial by an impartial jury trial' meant at the time….whether it's the common law, state practices in the founding era, or opinions and treatises…. the answer is unmistakable. A jury must reach a unanimous verdict in order to convict."

"What do you think of that?" he asked Katz.

"I think it's a good decision," Katz said. He enjoyed talking to the law student. And the call was well timed. Katz needed a diversion from his conversation with Ryan Long. For a minute, he put on his law professor's hat and said, "Unanimity does many things. Sometimes it requires compromise. It ensures that different theories of a case are evaluated. Sometimes those theories are diametrically opposed to one another. And it enables jurors to present a united front, which may be important in a tough criminal case or a substantial money judgment in a civil proceeding."

"I agree with everything you said," Reese replied.

"But," Katz cautioned, "unanimity can also subvert the system."

"What do you mean?"

Katz studied Reese on the screen. He was young and idealistic. He and Lin had just started a family and their entire life was in front of them.

"What is the single most important thing in a criminal case, or, for that matter, in any case, civil or criminal?" Katz asked Reese.

"The presentation of evidence," Reese replied without hesitation. "To be sure that you provide evidence that covers every element of the offense."

"Yeah, well, that's important, but that's a textbook response," Katz said. "If you don't present evidence, your case is going to fold somewhere along the line, either at a motion to strike, during jury deliberation, or on appeal. But assume you have the evidence you need to sustain a conviction. What else?"

"Is this a trick question?"

"No, it's not a trick question," Katz replied dismissively.

"The opening statement," Reese said.

"Now you're guessing," Katz said. "Neither the opening statement nor the closing argument is evidence; judges instruct juries not to regard them as such. Lawyers have the power to persuade and I've seen attorneys create narratives diametrically opposite from the evidence presented at trial, and win."

"You were once one of them."

"I still am," Katz corrected him. Then he answered the question: "The most important part of the trial is *voir dire*, the selection of the jury. And that takes me back to my earlier statement about unanimous juries and how the system can be subverted. You see, David, a single juror can thwart the good intentions of 11 other people just like a discordant note can destroy a beautiful melody."

He continued, "The key of *voir dire* is to identify the outlier. If that person is going to prevent you from attaining your desired outcome — either because he's altruistic or sinister — you have to strike him from the jury. Conversely, if that person is going to bring about your desired outcome — either steer the jury to the preferred verdict or be the sole holdout forcing a hung jury — then you have to allow that the juror to remain on the panel.

"You have to identify that person at the outset of the case right away. You have to have the right people on the jury panel or excluded from it. If you succeed there, you stand a good chance of winning. But if you fail, you lose, even if you're holding the winning hand.

"They don't teach you that in law school. But every good prosecutor and defense attorney knows it's true. In the end, you play the odds."

Chapter Two: STONE

"I DESPAIR. Jane is suffering. I feel it in my bones. I suppose it should not be surprising that I should feel her pain. I sense things tightening each night. Life is departing from my side. Are you? I hope not. My action was intended to benefit both of us. It seems to have hurt us instead. Death seems close by. I have suicidal tendencies. If I am suspected of her assault, I don't know what I'm going to do. However it plays out, we are in it together. I would not have acted as I did without your encouragement. It was quiet encouragement, but I know you agreed with my decision. You knew it was going to happen. I cannot share your love with another woman. I need you for myself. All of you."

*

KATZ CALLED Stone and asked to meet her at Hutton's residence. He said he'd explain when he saw her. When she arrived, he was standing on the front walk. He wore a cloth mask and latex gloves and held two papers in his hands. They were the blowups of the images in Hutton's kitchen that Shorter sent him.

Stone was dressed all in black, including her mask and gloves. Looking at her approach, Katz thought that she looked a little like a gunslinger. She disregarded social distancing and walked right up to him. He handed her the papers.

"These are close-ups of the countertops in Jane's kitchen," he explained. "There's a digital assistant speaker on the counter." He pointed it out to her. "I want to check the make and model of the device. It should be taken into custody. We'll need a warrant to conduct a search of her online account. It'll take time but it might shed some light on what happened at the time of the murder."

"There wasn't one of these devices on the counter," Stone said.

"That's impossible," Katz replied.

Stone ripped the yellow tape and unlocked the door. Together they entered the home. Nothing had been disturbed since the afternoon of the attack. Blood had dried on the wood floor in the foyer and on the tiles in the kitchen. Katz glanced at the kitchen counter. He moved a chair and stood where Hutton would have been seated during the video conference calls. His eye was drawn to the tile floor.

He held up the two photos, one in each hand. "You're right," he said. "It's not here."

Stone surveyed the counters and then looked at the photos. "I'm not surprised," she said. "I would have noticed it if it had been here." She looked carefully at the countertop. "There's nothing to suggest that it was taken at the time of the attack," she continued. "It could have been moved at any time. When did you conduct the video call?"

"About a month ago," Katz said. "March 18." He walked back to the front door. He reimagined the attack. "Jane opens the door and is immediately attacked. She falls backwards onto the kitchen floor. She yells out to the device. Maybe she tells it to call 911." He walked back into the kitchen and placed the photos on the counter. He glanced pointedly at the floor, then turned his eyes to Stone. She met his glance.

"But there was no 911 call," she said. "I checked. We would have kept a record if a call had come into the station. EMTs would have been dispatched immediately to the house. None of that happened."

"Maybe she simply called out the name of her assailant," Katz said.

"Let's assume that's what happened," Stone said, playing along.

"Suppose the machine didn't turn on?" Katz asked rhetorically. "Suppose she was too weak to call out? If that was the case, the assailant might have been spooked. She might have been afraid that Jane would call out again for help. All Jane had to do was summon 911 and there would have been a team here within minutes. There's a firehouse literally around the corner."

"You said *she*," Stone said. "Do you still think the attacker was a woman?"

"Nothing definitive, but yes."

"Interesting."

Katz continued with his analysis. "Another possibility is that Jane might have alerted her machine and identified the name of her assailant rather than call for help. The transcript would permanently log that name in her account. If we saw the device, it would only be a matter of time before we accessed the account and discovered the name of the attacker.

"So the attacker had to get rid of the device. If there was no evidence of the device, no one would bother to check any record."

Stone nodded in agreement. "It makes sense, Mo. All we have to do is locate the device and we have our prime suspect, assuming that Jane actually called out something." Then she addressed the 100-pound gorilla in the room. "I saw you glance at that tile a minute ago," she said. "I omitted calling it to your attention when we were previously at the house."

It was a smart choice of words, Katz thought. She had not simply omitted it; she had deliberately hidden it from him. Yet he trusted her and realized there was no need at this point to argue about her choice of words. "So what is it?" he asked.

It was a heel mark.

"It was dipped in Hutton's blood," Stone said.

"You mean someone stepped in Jane's blood and left a mark," he corrected her.

"No, Mo, I mean what I said. Someone dipped the heel of a boot in her blood." She grabbed and removed her mask. "I hate this damn thing," she said. Katz unfastened his mask as well. Stone continued, "The print was made with a rubber heel from one of those duck shoes, like the kind L.L. Bean makes, except it wasn't their brand." She shrugged. "We already checked."

"What leads you to that conclusion?" As he asked the question, his mind raced forward with the implications of the statement and the reason that Stone had withheld the information from him.

"The instant I saw it, I knew it was too perfect. A rubber heel would have left a scuff mark. The heel would have slipped. It would have been next to the blood. There would have been more than one mark. And the assailant would have cleaned up the evidence. All those things led me to the same conclusion, namely that someone planted that print for us to find it."

Katz trusted her deductive reasoning and said so with his eyes.

"Come with me," she said. They went to the basement. "I know what you're thinking," Stone said, leading the way. "You're thinking the assailant could have removed the boots after noticing blood on them. Hence, the absence of additional prints on the rug." She opened the sliding glass door and they stepped onto the patio. Orange cones surrounded a patch of grass and mud abutting the patio bricks. "Except there was another print here."

Katz looked at it. "The attacker removed the boots upstairs and put them back on before going outside."

"Unlikely," she said. "This print is from the same shoe as the blood. It's the front end of the shoe. The print is planted in an area that was protected from last Sunday's rain. Someone pressed that boot into the ground just like they dipped the boot into the blood. They fabricated evidence."

"And why did you withhold it from me?"

"For the same reason you are." She met his stare and he turned away. "I know you're conducting a bit of a sidebar investigation." She smiled slyly. "You can fool everyone else, Mo, but you can't fool me. I recognize your tricks because we're cut from the same cloth. And I'll tell you something else. I think we both have the same suspicion. Let's leave it there for now, okay?"

"Fair enough," he replied.

They returned upstairs.

"Have you spoken to Tricia Barton?" asked Katz.

"Not yet," Stone replied. "It's my understanding she was rushed to the hospital Sunday afternoon. Depending on what time it was, it could be a legitimate alibi."

"Or an incriminating piece of evidence," Katz said.

"There are always at least two ways to look at everything," she said.

They called the hospital. It took a considerable amount of time to be connected to someone in the medical records department. Under normal circumstances, the hospital would have required a subpoena before releasing any information. But these were not normal times. The hospital understood that efforts were underway to solve Jane Hutton's attack. The information requested by the U.S. Attorney and the Alexandria police officer seemed reasonable, and it was anyone's guess how long it would take to go the route of a subpoena.

"The patient checked in on Sunday night a little after 5 p.m.," the hospital representative said. "She claimed to be suffering from symptoms synonymous with COVID-19. Headaches, body aches, loss of taste, difficulty breathing, and fever. You know the drill. Fortunately, we could not confirm any medical issues and she was discharged on Monday. She never ran a fever and she tested negative for the virus."

Katz and Stone compared notes after the call ended. Katz was suspicious. He concluded that Barton might have deliberately checked herself into the hospital to create an alibi. Stone said it was a possibility but it was inconsistent with her own theory of the case. Despite their difference of opinion, they concurred on a course of action.

"You still questioning our theory that it's a woman?" Katz asked as they left for Barton's place.

Stone didn't answer him.

*

TRICIA BARTON'S townhouse was seven blocks away. While Stone drove, Katz did a quick conference call to Lin, McCarthy, and

Santana. Two of the three answered. He told them about the device missing in the kitchen.

Stone double-parked in front of Barton's townhouse. All of the parking spaces were taken. Cars were covered with spring pollen. No one had driven in days. Stone kept her emergency equipment on, but the street was deserted.

They exited the vehicle together and walked up the drive. Stone placed a hand on her service weapon as she knocked on the front door. Katz stood slightly behind her. He had heard about instances where suspects fire bullets indiscriminately through doors when police officers approach. He did not want to become a casualty of such an incident.

No one answered. Stone knocked again. "Alexandria police," she hollered. "Open up." She removed her gun, took a step back, and busted open the door with her heavy boot. She went in first, Katz behind her. "Stay here," she instructed him. "Let me conduct a sweep first." With her gun drawn in front of her, Stone moved briskly across the main floor. Then she went upstairs. She came down, swept across the main floor again, and went into the basement. A second later, she called to Katz. "Come down here."

Katz ran down the stairs to the basement. He rushed by an office and utility room to a family room. A fireplace was located against the far wall. To its left was the sliding glass door; to the right, a large ceiling-to-floor window. A small gold candelabra was located on the mantle above the fireplace. A sofa and two chairs were on either side of a coffee table.

Barton was lying next to a coffee table. Her head rested in a pool of blood. A trickle of blood ran from her temple to the puddle of blood. A revolver was pressed in her hand. The elbow of the arm holding the gun was cocked at an angle pointed at her head. Her eyes were open. The acrid smell of gunpowder and fresh blood permeated the room.

A digital assistant was located in the center of the coffee table.

A cell phone was positioned beside it. The room was quiet, like a morgue.

Stone was already summoning the EMTs. "We have a victim of an apparent suicide," she said. She provided the address. Then she called the police station and ordered uniforms to the scene. When she finished, she surveyed the room. "Looks as though she sensed someone closing in on her," she said.

Katz detected a touch of skepticism in her voice.

Stone swept the house again to see if anyone was inside. Katz remained downstairs. By the time she finished, uniforms had arrived along with an ambulance. To avoid contaminating any evidence, Katz went outside. Stone remained inside with the officers.

Santana arrived at the scene. He donned a mask as he stepped out of his car, then joined Katz on the drive. He was dressed in grey sweatpants and a blue sweatshirt. "How tragic," he said. "I wonder if it's connected to the coronavirus. She might have had it."

Katz disabused him of any such thought. "She never had COVID-19," he said. "She checked herself into the hospital claiming to have a fever and other symptoms but was discharged the following morning. Arguably, she used the virus as an alibi."

Santana raised his eyebrows.

"People are using this pandemic to profit every way they can," Katz said.

"It's pathetic," Santana commented. "To think the whole thing was a ruse on her part. She basically took a ride in an ambulance to escape the crime scene."

"You're assuming she's responsible," Katz said.

Santana looked at Katz. "WTF, Mo. Yeah, I'm assuming she's responsible. The woman just blew her brains out." As he spoke, the EMTs departed the house with the stretcher. Santana and Katz stepped aside to give them room. He lowered his voice to a respectful level. "What else do you think compelled her to do something like this? I only wish we had gotten here sooner. She was on our radar.

Maybe we were delinquent in finding and interviewing her."

Stone came outside. She put her arm around Santana's waist. "Want to come inside?" she asked. As they entered, she said, "This woman was like a duplicate copy of her daughter. Even the house. Look around."

For the first time, Katz focused on the house's layout. It was an exact replica of Hutton's home. Since he had just departed Hutton's home with Stone, Katz had a clear picture in his mind of both houses.

"The houses were both built at the same time in the 1800s by the same contractor," Stone said.

"How do you know that?" Katz asked.

"Reese looked it up," she answered. "He was doing a virtual walk around the neighborhood. He noticed it and did a little research. The architect was a member of the Daingerfield family, one of the original settlers of Alexandria. It's the mirror reflection of Hutton's place, inside and out, down to the smallest detail."

Katz stopped in the kitchen. The room was identical to the kitchen in Hutton's house. The same items were arrayed on the countertops, except in opposite order: toaster, cutlery set, pepper grinder, coffee bean grinder, espresso machine, coffee maker, pewter cup, cheese grater shaped like the Eiffel Tower, salt and pepper shakers, and large vase containing mixing spoons. Between the cup and the cheese grater was a digital assistant.

"This is freaky," Santana said.

"Do you see what I see?" Katz asked Stone.

"I do," she said. They told Santana about the digital assistant. "There's a digital assistant in the basement," she said. "I'm sure it belongs to Hutton. The implication is that Barton took it after she attacked her daughter for fear Hutton would call 911 for help."

"It may take some time to crack the password," Santana said.

Stone looked at Katz, cocked her eyebrows, and said, "It's not going to take any time at all. I'm going to guess the password is 'Tricia.' Weird, but probably true."

Santana said, "It's more than weird."

"Pray tell," Stone said.

"I'm no psychologist, but somewhere along the line Barton recognized that her daughter was more successful than she was," Santana said. "Barton started imitating her daughter to catch up with her. That turned into an obsession. Then the mother tried to outdo the daughter. It morphed into a sick competition."

They also noticed an empty slot in the wooden set of cutlery. A knife was missing.

A few minutes later, they went back outside. More cruisers arrived, along with two news vans. A reporter emerged from one of the vans, along with another man with a camera slung over his shoulder. Both were wearing masks with the logo of the local television station. It took a few minutes to get set before the reporter broadcast his story on air.

"Moments ago, the body of Alexandria socialite and Washington icon Tricia Barton was discovered in the basement of her home. The house is located around the corner from the home of Barton's daughter, Jane Hutton, who was attacked on Easter Sunday. Hutton is reportedly at Johns Hopkins hospital in serious condition, compounded by a positive test for COVID-19. There is no word yet as to whether Barton's suicide is linked to Hutton's attack. We'll be bringing you details as they become available."

The reporter put down his microphone and walked over to Stone, Katz, and Santana. "How's everyone doing?" he asked. He was tall, lanky, with wavy dark hair. He was dressed in slacks and an open-necked shirt. "Tom Mann, *On the Spot News*." He nodded to Stone, whom he recognized. He extended his elbow toward Stone and she awkwardly extended hers. "Any comment?"

"Not yet," Stone said. "Too soon. We'll issue a statement when we have more details to release."

"What about the emails?" he asked. "I understand Ms. Barton wrote to her lover. Any comment about those?"

159

"Who told you that?" Santana interjected.

Mann looked at him coolly. "Confidential," Mann replied. "You all know how that works. If we revealed our sources we'd never get any information."

"By the way, who are you?" he asked. Stone made introductions, emphasizing that Santana and Katz were invested in finding out who had attacked their colleague, Jane Hutton.

Returning to the topic at hand, the reporter said, "For what it's worth, I understand Barton incriminated herself in the emails."

Before they had time to digest that information, McCarthy rode up on a bicycle. "I heard the news," he said, joining the foursome standing on the drive. He had on a mask and wore sweatpants and a T-shirt. Mann extended his elbow as Stone introduced them. They tapped. "How did it all go down?" McCarthy asked the group.

Stone was careful in what she said in Mann's presence. "Mo and I dropped over to talk to Tricia Barton. No one answered. I broke down the door. We found her in the basement. No one else was in the residence. We're waiting for forensics to complete their work." She looked at Mann. "This is not for attribution."

"You didn't say anything," he shot back. Nonetheless, he nodded his consent.

The group broke up. Katz accompanied Stone to her cruiser. She turned off the emergency lights, which had been flashing across Barton's front yard for the past 45 minutes. They drove back to Hutton's place, where Katz had left his car.

Katz asked Stone if she had any doubts about whether Barton had taken her own life.

"I'll let forensics decide that, but you know how I feel," she said. "There was no reason for her to take her own life. There's no suicide note."

"What else?"

"That digital assistant device and phone looked to me as though they were planted by someone. They were right out in the open beside the body waiting to be found. If a pair of boots are in the closet with blood on the heel and mud on the sole, that'll seal the deal for me."

"You really think this is a setup?"

"Think, Mo? You and I both have our suspicions. Don't play coy with me. I've known you too long. Plus we're both cut from the same cloth."

As they pulled up in front of Hutton's place, Katz said, "Listen, it's late and neither of us expected any of this to happen. Why don't you drive over to my place and join Abby and me for dinner? We can invite Curtis to join us."

*

ANOTHER EMAIL, sent two hours earlier.

"I'm so sorry for dragging you into this mess. I acted for love. Only for love. For us! Only for us. But now everything is turning out wrong. I never wanted to hurt you, my darling. I feel as though I am infected with the coronavirus. It is affecting my actions and my thoughts. Dark thoughts. They lurk in the recesses of my mind. I feel at times as though I am going mad. Why haven't you come to see me? I expected you the other night. I left the door open. I will leave it open again tonight. I cannot bear to be alone. Not now. Come to me, my sweet. If you fail to come, I may do something desperate. I will not be separated from you. Not now. If this is the end, I am counting on you to hide anything that can incriminate me. Destroy my shoes. Destroy it all. Death and destruction befit me. Oh, what am I saying. I don't want to sound melodramatic. I don't want to do anything drastic. I just want you. It's all I've ever wanted. She never deserved you. You belong to me. Only to me. Now and forevermore."

*

SNOWE HAD taken leftovers out of the refrigerator when Stone and Katz came in. While Katz parked three blocks away,

Stone double-parked in front of his house, turned on the emergency equipment and waited for him. "Just in time for dinner," Snowe said. "When I saw those lights flashing and Sherry in the car, I set the table for three."

They sat in the living room, maintaining social distance. Katz was on the sofa, Snowe in an easy chair in the far-left corner of the room, and Stone in a chair in the right corner. To date, none of them exhibited any signs of COVID-19 — no coughing, congestion, or fever — and each of them doubted the other carried the virus. But Katz had been outside today for the first time in a week. Stone disregarded the warnings about staying indoors and had been reporting to the station each day during April. None of them wanted to risk someone else's health. Katz already planned to sleep in a separate room tonight as a precaution. It bordered on the bizarre and the incomprehensible, but here they were, silent and fearful, sitting six feet apart from each other.

"Despite your skepticism, let's assume Tricia Barton attacked Jane," Katz said to Stone. "Why would she do it? What was the motive?"

"They shared a love interest," Stone said.

"How did you come to that conclusion?"

"You talk about *me* withholding evidence from you! McCarthy interviewed a woman from the townhome association several days ago who had all the gossip about some guy who was screwing both of them. He never told me about it. I had David Reese track her down.

"She gushed like a fire hydrant. She told him her life history along with the life histories of Jane Hutton, Tricia Barton, and everyone else who lives within three miles of Slaters Lane."

"Does she know the name of their love interest?" Katz asked.

"No," answered Stone. "And that's a problem. He did a good job of hiding his identity. He only visited Jane on weekends. And it appears the only times he met Barton was either on his way to or from Jane's place. You can talk about the mother and daughter being strange for dressing like one another and living in mirror reflections of each other's home. This guy was part of that weirdness. He was the most dangerous part."

"You should interview the fire hydrant again," Katz said. "I'll bet you she knows even more than she's admitting."

His phone chirped. Lin was texting. He texted back to suggest a quick video conference with McCarthy and Santana. Lin said she could join in about 15 minutes. Katz sent out an email to the group with a link to the call.

"Do you want Curtis to come over and join us here?" Katz asked Stone.

"No, he's gotten used to seeing us more on screens than in person," she said. "I think he likes it. He's a 60-feet-of-separation kind of guy. Sort of a Larry David type."

As they waited for the group call, Katz asked Stone, "So what's your point about the man who was having a relationship with both women?"

"I think he recognized their weakness and exploited it," she said. "Sort of like becoming the human coronavirus. He preyed on two women who were locked in some sort of strange competition with one another. That was their pre-existing condition and he took advantage of it. When we finally resolve this case, we're going to discover he played a role in both Jane's attack and Barton's apparent suicide."

Stone shared her hypothesis with the others during their call, which was conducted primarily to update Lin, since both Santana and McCarthy had shown up at Barton's house. When Stone finished, Katz said, "Our primary focus is finding this man. He's the linchpin. He may know whether Barton attacked Jane and, if so, why she tried to kill her own daughter. He may also have answers as to why Barton took her own life."

The call ended. Stone stayed until late in the evening. The case was moving to a place where the prime suspect was coming clearly into focus. Within a short time, they both knew they would arrest the man who was having sexual relations with both women.

*

Wednesday, April 10

HUTTON CYCLED to the park and stopped. People were out walking their dogs. Some were standing along the shoreline where the park abutted the water and looked out onto the Potomac River. A few sailboats dotted the water. Was it her imagination or were the sails all practicing social distancing as well? She chuckled to herself as she turned and saw him approaching.

She would have been devastated if she knew that Mike McCarthy was also having sex with her mother. The possibility was too absurd to enter her mind. But if she had bothered to study his background, she might have seen it.

McCarthy and Tricia Barton began their relationship while McCarthy was a congressional aide to Abe Lowenstein. McCarthy was a nobody. Barton was entwined in highly publicized relationships with the likes of Hank Simon. But Simon was boring and clumsy. McCarthy, on the other hand, was a young and vibrant Hill staffer. She enjoyed sharing her bed with him, although they had to do so in secret. The secrecy became a sort of obsession, and they had successfully kept it under wraps for six years.

"Hey, beautiful," McCarthy said as he stopped his bicycle beside Hutton's. Together they pedaled to the shoreline. They were both wearing masks. Between the facial coverings and their helmets, no one could identify either of them.

"Do you know Suzanne Marconi?" she asked.

"I do," he replied. "She's chairman of BOM. I never met her, but I remember her name on court filings from last year. Why?"

"I got a letter from a whistleblower about her," Hutton said. "In addition to being chairman of BOM, she's a successful businesswoman in her own right. She operates several businesses that contract with the public and private sectors to clean buildings. She subcontracts with a company headquartered in Paterson, New Jersey."

"What was the complaint about?"

"Ostensibly about a guy named David Simon. He and Marconi are engaged in a scheme to skim money off the top of their contracts. They basically enter into the same contract with two separate parties. It's been going on for years. Simon gets a federal or state contract. He subcontracts to Marconi. At the same time, she contracts with a private company for the same work, probably the tenant."

"That's unbelievable," he said. "You seem to know a fair amount about it."

"I know Simon. He was a client at Stephens Babcock. I dated him once. Just for a little while. He's an asshole. All he's ever wanted to do was make a fast buck. He's always felt overshadowed by his uncle, a guy named Hank Simon.

"I had a premonition I'd see more of his cases after I arrived in the U.S. Attorney's office. I actually copied of some of the firm's cases and brought them with me when I came over to your office. I knew I wasn't supposed to. I just want to be able to compare his footprint the next time I see it. That way I can advise attorneys how to avoid pitfalls, craft a winning offense, and defeat the tactics previously used to win acquittals."

"Sounds pretty sinister to me," he smiled. "Do I detect a little bit of a desire to get some personal revenge as well against an undeserving suitor? And maybe payback against Marconi?"

"Maybe," she smiled coyly. "Next week, I'm going to do a comparative analysis between the facts alleged in the complaint and the methodology that Simon and Marconi employed in the previous cases. I'm going to sketch out a winning strategy and recommend a formal complaint be lodged by our office. It sure looks to me like a criminal fraud case.

"If you like, I'll give you the letter. I'm going to go into the office tomorrow to pick up some other files and books. If you want to meet, I can give it to you."

"Let's do that," he said. "What about the thumb drive?"

"Mai Lin has it. She keeps it locked in her credenza at the office."

They watched the sailboats. Dusk turned to night. They cycled to her home.

*

SHORTLY AFTER Stone departed, Katz went outside to take a walk. The air was cool and damp. Everywhere he turned, he was greeted by neighbors he had never seen before. An old man with white hair and a week's growth of grey beard on his wrinkled jowls waved as he rode by on a bicycle. Couples and entire families strolled together as though on an evening promenade somewhere in Italy. Stuffed bears, part of a children's "bear hunt" game, looked out from upstairs windows of homes or between the branches of trees. Painted rocks adorned street corners and the edges of yards in another game.

His personal phone rang. He looked at the number and braced himself. "Hey, Pops," he said.

"I wanted you to know that your mother's been released from the hospital. She's self-quarantined in her room. She's weak and she's going to have to be closely monitored, but she's home." His voice quivered. "She's back home with me, son."

"I'm so happy to hear that."

"*You're* happy!" his father replied. "I'm thrilled. I'm going to make her a bleach bath tonight." He laughed. "Seriously, I'm going to take care of her and avoid doing anything crazy in terms of treatment. She's on some medications. People will come to the house and check on her. And I think she will participate in some sort of study. To be honest, I'm a little hard of hearing and there was so much excitement today that I'm not sure I heard everything that was said, plus I'm even less certain that I heard it correctly. But she's home and that's the important thing."

Myron Katz sounded giddy.

Katz smiled. He had come to an intersection along King Street. He stopped. There was no one coming in any direction. It was eerie. Somewhere in the distance, a bus lumbered along King Street. That was the only sound of traffic.

"That's just great, Pops. Tell her I love her. I'd like to get up to see you soon."

"Around Thanksgiving," his father said. "That would probably be good. We should have the all-clear sign by then, I hope. But who knows? The numbers are starting to come down in New York, or at least they've plateaued, or so they say. But who knows what's going to happen in the heartland?" He laughed again. "I'm just relieved. You have no idea."

"I'm relieved too. I'll call you back in about a week or so."

*

KATZ WAS on an emotional high. Being reunited with his parents removed a psychological barrier that was lodged deep in his soul. It was like the healing of a wound. Just as his mother faced a perilous condition and survived, he felt as though he'd been carrying a similar sickness for years. He appeared asymptomatic, so to speak, even though he would have tested positive if someone could have taken the temperature of his psyche. Now they were all on the road to recovery, physically and psychologically.

The euphoria would be short-lived. Perhaps it was a sign of the times, Katz thought after he took the next phone call. At one end of the spectrum, there was hope and survival. At the other end, devastation and sorrow. In the scope of a few minutes, he experienced both of them.

"Mr. Katz, I'm calling from Johns Hopkins in Baltimore," the voice on the phone said. He recalled the cadence. It was the same doctor with whom he had spoken on the 12th. "Jane Hutton died a short while ago."

Katz closed his eyes and pressed his thumb and fingers over his eyelids like he was squeezing lemons; tears slowly seeped down his cheek. He had crossed the intersection. Fortunately, there was a bench near the corner because he suddenly felt the need to sit down. Just a few yards down the block, he saw two elderly men wearing protective masks and playing chess.

"I'm sorry to bring you such sad news," the doctor continued. "We were unable to find any immediate family members. We thought it best to contact you."

Katz asked when Hutton had died. It occurred to Katz that she might have expired at about the same time as her mother would have succumbed from a fatal bullet to the head. The medical examiner's record would confirm that the time was within the hour.

"What can you tell me about what happened?" he asked.

"She never regained consciousness following the surgery. The loss of blood was substantial. Then she tested positive for the coronavirus. Her body went into overdrive trying to compensate. It only weakened her further. All of her major arteries shut down. We did everything we could. She was placed on a ventilator but by then it was already too late.

"If it's any consolation to you, she died the same way she lived her life, at least from what I've heard about her. She went out a fighter."

Katz stayed on the line with the doctor for another 20 minutes. He wanted to hear about how she fought to stay alive. As he listened, he felt a closeness to Hutton and to her mother. He sensed that they were close by, just around the corner, down Slaters Lane.

"Okay, thank you," Katz said when there was nothing more to learn. "We'll be in touch to make necessary arrangements for her."

Katz sat on the bench for a long time. The sound he heard was the sound of silence. He tried to recall the lyrics to the Simon and

Garfunkel song, *The Sound of Silence*. That line about darkness being an old friend kept repeating in his mind like a broken record, over and over. He couldn't concentrate. He stared at the two men playing chess. Finally, they stopped and stared back at him. He waved his apology for intruding on their meditation, stood up, and started back home.

He had just spoken with his team, but now he had to reassemble them again. He had grim news to share. He also needed to bring the search for the mysterious male companion to end game. Two people had been lost, one of whom was a close member of his staff. If his suspicion was correct — and he was confident it was the same suspicion shared by Stone — he was about to lose another member of his inner circle. Except in this case, the damage had been self-inflicted.

*

THE VIDEO conference started. Only Lin and Santana were on the line. "Where's Mac?" Katz asked. Nobody knew. "Okay," Katz said, placing his palm on his forehead as if checking for a fever. "I got a call from the doctor in Baltimore. Jane is dead. The doctor said she went down as a fighter."

Silence pervaded the call. It sounded just like the silence that engulfed Katz in the park. Hello to darkness.

A moment later, another screen appeared on the computer. Sherry Stone was joining the conversation. David Reese was seated beside her.

Katz quickly relayed the news about Hutton.

"Okay," Katz said. "We have a job to do and we need to get started. I don't think Mac is going to join us, to be honest. I think he might be implicated in this thing and that he might be on the run." As Katz looked at the screen, Lin's and Santana's facial expressions registered disappointment and sadness. Neither of them appeared entirely surprised. "For the past several days, Sherry's been running down leads. Let me turn this over to her."

Stone pushed her chair forward and leaned into the computer screen. "It may come as a surprise to you, but Mac and Tricia Barton were a couple. It was supposedly a secret. Very few people even suspected it. It was not the kind of news that got publicized, like the fact that Barton was involved with Hank Simon. But if you search on the internet long enough, like David did, you find stuff."

Reese shared his discoveries. "Barton met Mac while he was working in the Senate for Abe Lowenstein. Mac was smitten. Given the age disparity — he's in his 40s and she was hitting 70, if she wasn't over it — they kept their relationship secret from the outside world.

"Rumors circulated last fall after the party for Hutton at Principle Gallery. She and Mac had a series of little tête-à-tête things off to the side throughout the evening. But those rumors died off. Mac and Barton were masters of discretion."

Santana and Lin had both been at the party. They thought back to the event.

McCarthy swept in between Barton and Hutton. "It's hard to tell the two of you apart," he said, putting one arm around Hutton and the other around Barton. "Actually, to be honest, Jane, you look like the older sister." Barton squeezed his arm and said, "I'll keep this one."

"All along, it was right in front of everyone," Santana said. "And nobody saw it."

"At some point, Jane Hutton must have seen it," Katz interjected.

"That's right," Stone said. "Hutton probably observed it at the party. She was always very competitive with her mother. I mean, they were competitive to a fault. Hutton became obsessed about wooing Mac away from her mother to demonstrate some sort of superiority."

There was a knock on Katz's front door. He interrupted Stone. "This might be a guy from the IG's office," he said. "I haven't shared this with any of you, but there are complaints about the amount of time we've been spending on Hutton's case. Some people are apparently pissed off about it."

His comment was met with a series of guffaws. "I need to get the door," he continued. "Assuming it's the guy from the IG's office — his name is Ryan Long — I'm going to ask him to sit here, in front of the computer." He pointed toward another chair that no one could see. "You can all watch us. It's going to be a show." Katz minimized the video images and opened his emails on the screen to disguise the fact that the video was open. "He'll never know you're watching." He placed the other chair beside his chair. "How's this?"

Lin said she could not see the other chair. There was another knock on the door. Katz adjusted the chair and the laptop, seeking the right angle. "That's perfect," Lin said.

Katz left the kitchen table and went to the front door. Without looking through the peephole, he opened the door. As he did so, it occurred to Katz how easy it was to open a door without suspecting there was danger on the other side of it. His hand turned the knob and the door swept open. The visitor moved forward. Katz stepped back, surprised and alarmed.

*

One Hour Earlier

ABRAHAM LOWENSTEIN opened the door to his home off Spout Run in Arlington. The address was stenciled in white letters on a black mailbox at the end of a stovepipe driveway that hid the house from the street. Mac McCarthy stood there. His hair was mussed. His face was ashen. His eyes were red. He looked as though he had not eaten in days.

"Can I come in?" McCarthy asked. The senator opened the door and look a step back. Even without guidance about social distancing, Lowenstein would not have embraced him. He looked sickly. McCarthy lowered his head. "I made a terrible decision," he said. "I abetted a crime. I've broken faith with my obligation to do the right thing in a moment of crisis."

They walked into the living room, decorated in a colonial style. Along the walls were photos of the senator with various well-known politicians and international dignitaries. Tip O'Neill, Anwar Sadat, Jimmy Carter, Bill and Hillary Clinton, Tony Blair, Al Gore, and Michael Dukakis.

"What the hell are you talking about?"

"Jane Hutton," McCarthy said. "I abetted her attack. I didn't know about it, I swear. Tricia Barton told me about it."

"Tricia? What in the name of God does she have to do with it?"

"She attacked her daughter, Abe."

Lowenstein was stunned. "How can I help you?" he asked. He didn't know what else to say. He was nervous. He had just heard the breaking news about Barton's suicide. The news that Hutton was dead was not yet public.

"I'd like you to contact Mo and explain the situation to him," McCarthy said. "I need to tell him that I never meant to bring any ill repute to his office. He's a proud man and he runs a tight ship. I never expected to be part of something like this. He's owed an explanation. I just don't feel capable of providing him with a coherent one."

"Mo Katz?" Lowenstein asked, incredulous. "You're involved in a malicious assault and you want me to contact Mo Katz so you can apologize?" It was insane request, Lowenstein thought. McCarthy should be turning himself in to the police. Katz had nothing to do with the prosecution of the case. It would be under the jurisdiction of the City of Alexandria.

"I can't do that," Lowenstein said. "And I'm not going to harbor you in my home either. You have to face this by yourself. You created this situation. There's no way you can explain your way out of it. But you might be able to come to terms with it yourself. You made your bed, Mac. You sleep in it."

"Please, sir," McCarthy begged. "I always did your bidding, Senator. When you wanted someone to keep you informed about the goings-on in the U.S. Attorney's office, I did as you requested, even when it compromised my loyalty to Katz. Now I'm asking for something in return. I just want you to convey my apologies."

"Not for me to do, and don't bother asking again. It's not going to change my mind. You'd better leave."

"I need your help."

"You're not going to get it! Don't you understand? You've admitted to me that you're involved in a brutal assault! I don't want to know the level of your involvement. I don't need to know the details. And I'm not going to talk to Mo Katz or anyone else about you. I won't be a character witness at your trial, either! If someone asks me, I'll tell them you're a no-good son of a bitch! Now turn around and get the hell out of my home. You have a lot of gall to come in here and talk as though I owe you a political favor. This isn't politics. This is a crime!"

*

THE EMAIL sat unread in the 'In' box. It had been composed shortly before Tricia Barton's death. The message was stuck in time as events continued to unfold.

"You now have all the details. You can go to the police if you want. I feel as though I have nothing to lose. Yet I also feel as though my own life is slipping away from me. I have suicidal thoughts. Did I ever tell you I suffer from depression and have had such inclinations in the past? Now they seem more real than ever. The walls are closing in around me. Society seems to be going off a cliff. I am in the front line. Do not desert me. I couldn't stand the strain entirely on my own."

Chapter Three: ST. VITUS' DANCE

"COME IN," Katz said. McCarthy bowed in thanks. He stepped into the dining room. Katz sat in the chair he had intended for Ryan Long. McCarthy sat at the head of the table. Katz positioned himself so that the laptop was directly between the two of them.

McCarthy was holding several papers, which he handed to Katz. "I want to confess to my involvement in Jane Hutton's attack," he said. "I'm complicit as an accessory after the fact."

Katz eyed the head of his criminal division with contempt. *Accessory after the fact.* It was as sad as it was ironic.

Katz scanned the papers.

"It's done. Don't hate me."

"I'm sorry for sending you such a curt email."

"I grow despondent. I now realize how little I meant to you."

"I despair. Jane is suffering. I feel it in my bones."

"I'm so sorry for dragging you into this mess. I acted for love. Only for love. For us!"

"What the hell is this?" Katz asked.

Without looking at Katz, McCarthy said, "I'd been having an affair with Jane." His head sank even lower. "And also with her mother. It had started to get out of hand. Tricia Barton wanted me to end the relationship with her daughter. Unfortunately, I was headed in the opposite direction. I was in the process of ending the relationship with her. Jane and I were going to move in together. Tricia went crazy.

"On Easter Sunday, she went to her daughter's house and attacked her. I didn't know anything about it, I swear. Afterwards, she confessed the crime to me. She started to send these emails to me. I should have reported it right away. I didn't. I can't hide the truth any longer, Mo. I know what I did was wrong. I'm prepared to suffer the consequences of my action."

He hid his face in his hands and started to cry.

"Look at me," Katz said. "Lift your head up and look at me."

McCarthy raised his head. Katz shifted his chair slightly. He glanced at the laptop.

"Did you play any role in planning and carrying out Jane's murder?"

"What? She's dead?"

"Yeah, she's dead. It's no longer an assault. It's now an act of cold-blooded murder."

McCarthy began to weep. "None, Mo. Honest. I didn't do anything until after it was over. Tricia never told me what she was planning. I only learned about it after the fact. I should have stepped forward. I failed everyone.

"And I feel responsible. Tricia acted because of my decision to leave her for Jane. Now she's taken her own life. And her daughter is dead. My whole world is crumbling. The whole coronavirus pales by comparison. I've suffered more harm and humiliation than I can stand."

Katz looked from McCarthy to the camera lens on the computer. "Anything else you want to say?"

"No, Mo. That's all. The emails tell the story. She sent them to me the past few days. As soon as I saw the first one, I knew. *It's done*, she wrote. I knew right away what she was talking about."

"Have you been back to Barton's house since then?"

"No, even though she's asked me to come over. She called me and asked me to take away some items from her home. A pair of boots. And something else, I forget. I didn't pay any attention. I was so angry with her. I was scared. I never went over to retrieve those items, like she requested. I never returned until I heard what she'd done to herself. That's when I biked over and met you and the others."

"I'm going to call Stone now," Katz said. "You're going to be taken into custody. You realize that the confession you just gave me is admissible in court?"

"I know."

Katz called Stone. She arrived at his house with four other officers. They handcuffed McCarthy and placed him in the back seat of a squad car. Everyone was wearing masks and latex gloves. Stone took possession of the emails. Katz told Stone about the boots. Stone said she would check to see if they had already been located at Barton's home.

*

REESE SHARED Stone's skepticism about Barton's culpability even before McCarthy confessed to Katz. As he watched McCarthy confessing to being an accessory after the fact, he put in a call to the forensic examiner. "I have a question about the wounds sustained by Jane Hutton," he said. "It's my understanding the wounds were superficial with the exception of the cut to the stomach."

"That's right," said the examiner.

"That's led some people to conclude the assailant lacked upper body strength, and that in turn has led to speculation that the suspect is most likely a woman."

"I suppose," said the examiner.

"But that's necessarily the case, is it?" asked Reese. "I mean, a man could have done it, too, right? Anyone could have deliberately struck a series of shallow wounds to trick us into believing it was more likely than not caused by a woman, right?"

"I don't know where you're going with that," said the examiner. "But yes, of course, those wounds could have deliberately been intended to simply cut the flesh. But why in the world would someone do that?"

*

FIFTEEN MINUTES after the police took McCarthy into custody, there was a knock on Katz's door. "There's a Ryan Long here to see you," Snowe said. Long was standing six feet behind her. He was tall and lanky, with pale skin and thinning hair. He had protuberant eyes over the mask that covered the lower half of his face. He waved with his right hand. He was wearing gloves. His left hand held a brown briefcase.

"Ryan," Katz said. "I expected you earlier. Please, sit down." Long sat at the opposite end of the table. "I haven't had time to assemble anything for you yet," Katz said.

"I'm concerned about your methods, Mr. Katz," Long said. His voice was cold and stern. He pulled out some papers from his briefcase and placed them the table.

"My methods?"

"Yes, Mr. Katz. I tried to get in touch with the complainant in your case and I've been unable to make contact. It's hard to get a handle on what's happening, but I hope you haven't retaliated against the complainant to silence him."

"I don't even know who filed the complaint, Ryan," Katz reminded him. "If you expect me to respond to your statement, I need to know who you're talking about. You mentioned you'd received complaints from people in my office and from city employees. Are you referring to someone in the federal or local workforce?"

Long cleared his throat. "There is only one complainant, and that individual is employed in your office. No one has complained from the city, at least not yet. I only mentioned the city because I fully expect complaints to be lodged because your heavy-handed approach violates city norms in conducting an investigation of this sort."

Katz nodded. "Are you going to share the name of the complainant?"

"Michael McCarthy."

Katz had suspected McCarthy all along, based upon the wording of the original email from Long. Snowe entered the dining room with two bottles of water. She smiled at Katz, who locked eyes but remained expressionless. She offered the water, which Katz took, but Long demurred.

Katz opened his bottle. "Well, I have to be honest with you," he said, taking a swig. "I do plan to take a series of administrative actions against Mac." Long clicked his pen. "He's going to be placed on administrative leave without pay. He will be removed him from his position as deputy U.S. Attorney. His PIV card will be revoked and his clearance terminated. He will be denied access to all federal facilities." Katz hesitated and then concluded, "I may have initiated some other administrative actions, but I can't think of them off the top of my head."

As Katz spoke, Long jotted down the laundry list of actions that had been initiated against McCarthy. It almost looked as though Long was salivating. He exhaled a deep breath. "Supervisors are not necessarily so forthcoming about the steps they've taken against subordinates who have initiated complaints against them, so I appreciate your candor," he said. "I also have to say I've never seen a supervisor act so forcefully against someone else in the office."

"Also, they're hauling Mac's ass off to jail," Katz said.

Long appeared confused. "Jail?"

"Yes. He confessed less than an hour ago to be an accessory after the fact to a murder."

Long froze. "You're kidding?"

"No," Katz said. "If you had been here an hour earlier, you would have witnessed his confession. He made it right here, in the same chair in which you're sitting."

Long stood up. He clicked his pen, tucked it in his pocket, and leaned over the table to close his notepad. "This really is quite remarkable. I mean, I don't know what to say."

Katz stood. It was no sign of disrespect that Katz did not shake hands with Long. Katz would have refrained even if the formality had not been eliminated due to the coronavirus. "You didn't write that email to me, did you, Ryan?" he asked. "Mac wrote it. I checked it against some of his other emails. The structure of the paragraph and the language. It's quintessential McCarthy. How did he persuade

179

you to send it to me?"

Long said nothing. "I have to go," he said.

"In fact, you're not even acting on behalf of the IG, are you? You did this as a favor to Mac. He asked you to intervene on his behalf. I don't know whether you knew he was trying to shut down our investigation into a crime in which he was involved, but that is in fact what he was doing." Katz looked hard at Long. "Do you understand the implications of what you've done?"

Long gulped. "I'll take that water," he said, looking sick. Katz retrieved the bottle and gave it to Long, whose hand was shaking as he accepted it.

"I could file a complaint with the IG," Katz said. "If I did, it would result in your being fired for acting outside of the scope of your position. Even worse than that, you could get implicated in Mac's effort to hide his criminality." Katz walked to the door and opened it. "I'm not sure what I'm going to do, Ryan." Long finished gulping the water and wiped his mouth against the back of his gloved hand. His eyes were filled with dread. "Don't you ever again abuse your authority or push your weight around like you tried to do with me, do you understand?"

"Yes, sir."

"The world is filled with disreputable people in positions of authority. Don't be one of them."

After Long departed, Katz returned to his computer. He was thinking about the email from Long that McCarthy had actually authored. He emailed Stone and Reese. "Is it possible Barton didn't write those notes to Mac?" he asked.

He got an immediate response. "Two steps ahead of you, Mo," Reese wrote. "I'm with Sherry at the station. I had doubts while I was watching the confession on the computer. We're working it now. We're in sync."

Katz nodded as he read the response, sensing where their inquiry was headed.

Snowe stole up behind him. "I made something for you," she said. She handed him a protective mask. "I made it from an old soccer shirt." It was a three-by-five-inch piece of heavy cotton fabric with pleats on either side so that it had a pouch in the middle and was narrower on the sides. Elastic loops were on either end to wrap the mask behind the ears.

He put it on. "This fits like a glove." He hoped the case against McCarthy fit as well.

*

Reese and Stone spent the night working. Lin was upset about Hutton's death and McCarthy's confession. She also did not want to spend the night alone. Despite guidance about the coronavirus, she and the baby went to Katz's and Snowe's home and spent the night in their guest bedroom. Santana spent the night alone at Stone's townhouse.

The group reassembled for a video conference in the morning. By that time, a search had been completed of Barton's home. A bloody, muddy boot was found in the closet, along with the personal digital assistant from Hutton's home. No murder weapon was recovered, but one of the knives from a set of cutlery was missing from the kitchen. Within a few days, the knives would be matched with the wounds sustained by Hutton to determine if her cuts originated from the same kind of item.

Despite a growing mountain of evidence, skepticism existed as to whether Barton had killed her daughter. Reese and Stone were together at the station. Lin was with Katz at his home. Everyone was in a separate room on a separate computer.

"This whole mother-daughter thing is bunk," Reese said. "They may have been competitive, but it never led the mother to kill her own daughter."

"What are you talking about?" Lin asked. "Mac already confessed to being an accessory after the fact. He's provided emails that Barton

181

sent to him after she attacked her daughter. It's an open-and-shut case."

"Don't you get it?" Reese pleaded. "Mac's whole confession was contrived. He's hoping we buy it hook, line, and sinker. He wants us to believe that Barton killed her daughter."

"That's insane," Lin said.

Katz studied Reese on the screen. It appeared that Reese's demeanor had changed from the naïve young man with whom he had recently discussed a Supreme Court decision. "Unpack it for us, David," Katz said. "Mac is a bit of a criminologist. He's also a good prosecutor. Maybe he's employing his talents to mislead and misdirect us."

"No doubt about it," Reese said. Stone gave a thumbs up on her screen. Reese said, "When Mac came to visit you, he immediately identified his role as being an accessory after the fact. Remember?" Katz nodded his head in affirmation. "Have either of you bothered to look up that offense?

"Don't answer, but I'm betting you didn't. It's 18 U.S.C. 3. And, Mo, while you probably know the elements of the offense and its penalty, let me read them to all of you." Reese raised a paper to his face and recited from the U.S. Code:

"Whoever, knowing that an offense against the United States has been committed, receives, relieves, comforts or assists the offender in order to hinder or prevent his apprehension, trial or punishment, is an accessory after the fact."

He put down the paper. "Think about that. Did Mac 'receive, relieve, comfort or assist' Barton after the fact?" He paused for half a second. "Maybe not. So, even though he said he was an accessory, he might be acquitted if he went to trial for the offense.

"But let's take the opposite position and assume he comforted her. Then consider the second element, which is that he assisted her 'in order to hinder or prevent her apprehension, trial, or punishment.' Do you think Mac did that?" He paused again. "It's an open question, isn't it?

"A jury is going to be unsure. Will that jury be unsure enough to acquit? Maybe. After all, the burden is *guilt beyond a reasonable doubt*. Mac received her emails, or so he claims. Having received those emails, he did nothing to hasten her apprehension."

Reese paused. He stroked his chin, rough like sandpaper from a few days' beard growth. "While you're pondering that, let me move on to the punishment phase," he continued. "Assume Mac is tried and convicted as an accessory after the fact, which is doubtful. Let me read the penalty to you. Oh, it's a little unique, so get ready." He picked up another piece of paper, held it close to his face, and read:

"Except as otherwise expressly provided by any Act of Congress, an accessory after the fact shall be imprisoned not more than one-half the maximum term of imprisonment or fined not more than one-half the maximum fine prescribed for the punishment of the principal, or both; or if the principal is punishable by life imprisonment or death, the accessory shall be imprisoned not more than 15 years."

Reese put down the paper. "In this case, Barton, the principal, is never going to be prosecuted because she's dead. So, if Mac was convicted, which I find unlikely, he could receive a much lighter sentence than might otherwise be the case."

"My point," Reese concluded, "is that Mac was never an accessory after the fact in connection with Jane Hutton's murder. He just wants us to believe he was. He surrendered himself to a lesser crime to avoid prosecution for the crimes he actually committed. He murdered Jane and made it look like it was Barton. Then he killed Barton."

Everyone was silent.

Stone added, "Plus, we just got some interesting film from one of Barton's neighbors who has a door camera. We'll tell you about it later."

The call ended. A little while later, Abe Lowenstein called Katz. He relayed that McCarthy had visited him and confessed to being an accessory. They agreed that McCarthy was searching for someone to whom he could confess the crime. When the senator threw him out, McCarthy came to Katz.

"Very strange cat," Lowenstein said.

"It's all part of his plan," Katz said, informing the senator about Reese's analysis. "When you think about it," Katz said, "Mac was stacking the deck in his favor by admitting to a crime before he was apprehended."

"It's more than strange," Lowenstein said. "It's diabolical. But why, Mo? Why would Mac do a thing like this?"

*

IT WAS EARTH DAY. Most of the news was related to the pandemic or the clean environment that had resulted from a total collapse of worldwide commerce and to the pandemic. There was also news about the apparent suicide of Tricia Barton.

After McCarthy had been booked as an accessory after the fact in Hutton's case, he was released on home detention. Despite the severity of the crime, the jail was flooded with inmates testing positive for the virus, and McCarthy did not appear to be a flight risk. By his own admission, his limited role was to assist Barton after she had murdered her daughter. And it was an open question whether he actually assisted her at all afterwards. There was no evidence that showed he was actively engaged in planning her murder.

Now, however, based on the analysis provided by Reese, squad cars pulled up outside McCarthy's home. They waited for the lead detective before entering. When Stone arrived, they followed her up the driveway. She was greeted at the door by Jimmy Wolfe, the debonair dean of the local defense bar. He was wearing a silk cravat as a mask.

"Can't say I'm surprised to see you here, Jimmy," Stone said. "Your client has been playing the game like a chess match."

Wolfe was nonplussed. "Let's get the ground rules set," he

said unceremoniously. "No search unless you have a warrant. No questioning of my client at this time, period. So, unless you've got grounds for his arrest, get out."

"We got it, Jimmy," she said. She handed Wolfe the warrant. She spoke to the officers behind her. "Place McCarthy under arrest for the murder of Tricia Barton." She turned back to Wolfe. "And this time there isn't going to be any release from custody after the booking process is completed."

"I trust you have more than nothing upon which to level these charges," Wolfe said as he stepped aside to let the officers enter the house.

Katz and Santana arrived. Everyone moved into the foyer. McCarthy appeared from another room. Everyone automatically spaced themselves several feet apart from one another.

"Yeah, I got probable cause," Stone said. "I just reviewed a tape that a neighbor recorded on her door cam. It shows your client walking across the street and entering Barton's home. He's carrying a bag. Twenty minutes later, he's seen leaving, but there's no bag. My theory is he went there with the digital assistant and a pair of boots, killed Barton, planted evidence, staged the scene, and left."

Wolfe stiffened. "What in the world are you talking about?" McCarthy remained expressionless. He simply looked at Stone, who avoided his gaze.

"Your client took a pair of shoes from Tricia Barton's home about a week before he killed Hutton. At the time, he wasn't sure whether or not he was going to get away with it or whether he was going to have to pin the murder on someone else. He didn't plan to take the digital assistant when he arrived. That just happened.

"Taking the device doesn't show a premeditated plan to frame her, but the shoes do. He took one of the shoes and dipped it in Hutton's blood. Then, when he opened the sliding glass door in the basement and went outside, he took the same boot and made a print in the mud.

"I saw the two prints when I first went to the house. You couldn't miss them. Same thing with the print on the patio. It was the sort of thing that a trial attorney dies for, no pun intended.

"When the shoe turned up as evidence, there was still blood on it. How was that possible? How could someone with blood on the heel of that shoe leave the house, step through the mud, run through the rain, and never wash off the blood from the heel of that shoe? The only way it could happen would be if the shoe was preserved after the heel was dipped in blood.

"And that's what Mac did. He put the shoe in the bag after he pressed the front end in the mud. He preserved it the same way a prosecutor would preserve evidence. Except he was preserving the evidence of his crime to convict his girlfriend."

"Why would he do something like that?" asked Wolfe.

"For the same reason he did everything else. To escape punishment. He covered every angle. One was for Barton to take the fall, with him pleading accessory after the fact knowing he had a chance of getting off at trial. Another was to kill her. I'm sure there were others. Unfortunately, he executed the kill option before we had a chance to stop him."

Wolfe said nothing. Stone nodded to the uniforms, who put McCarthy into handcuffs. McCarthy pleaded with his eyes for Wolfe to do something.

"You weasel," Stone said to McCarthy. "You lied to everyone, including us. You panicked when you learned that Kyle Judkis had seen you. I would have loved to have seen the expression on your face. There you were, gathering information about a crime you had committed and learning that a witness had seen you running between the two houses." She hesitated. "Screw the six feet." She got right in his face. "Did you squirm? She told me about how you had technical difficulty with the video. What a joke."

"Okay, Sherry," Katz said in a warning tone.

"It's not okay, Mo," she said. "It's totally not okay. He gathered that information from the blabbermouth at the homeowners association and hid it. He tried to manipulate it. He got her believing she might have seen Barton at her daughter's house. And he claimed he was going to protect her anonymity when all he wanted to do was keep her away from us. It's not okay. None of it was okay."

McCarthy looked at Wolfe. *Let her vent*, he said with his eyes. *It doesn't matter. The only thing that matters is how all of this plays in front of a jury. I'm a prosecutor. I know how it works. I know how I'm going to save myself. It's why I did everything the way I did.*

"I got your number, Mac," Stone said. "It was all staged. It reminded me of exhibits at a trial. I only wish I had made the connection to you at the time."

"I think you better take her outside," Katz said to Santana.

"No, please, let her stay," Wolfe said. "This is great discovery. She's sharing all the state secrets with me." He looked at Stone. "Please continue, detective. It's fascinating. Your powers of deduction are extraordinary."

"Fuck you!" Stone hollered. Santana took her by the elbow and pulled her toward the door.

On cue, an officer stepped into the foyer triumphantly holding up a burgundy-colored shopping bag with the star-studded logo of a brand department store. "Is that your evidence?" Wolfe scoffed. "Is that supposed to be the bag seen on the door cam? Those bags are ubiquitous. You're going to need a lot more than that if you intend to mount a case against my client."

The officer opened the bag. They all peered inside. A pair of latex gloves were rolled up in the bottom. Stone took a pen out of her pocket, hooked it under one of the gloves, and raised it out of the bag.

"Everyone is wearing gloves and masks when they go outside," Wolfe said. "I'd be surprised if I didn't see such items in handbags, shopping bags, and the like. It's hardly corroborating evidence of a crime."

"Not bad, Jimmy," Stone said. "You always were quick with an explanation. Unflappable whenever incriminating evidence was presented against one of your clients, as I recall. And you might be right. This could be coincidental, even though we both know it isn't. The proof will be whether there's a gunpowder residue inside that glove once they examine it. I don't think that's something that happens on a routine basis. And I'm willing to wager they're going to find blood and mud inside the bag."

Wolfe waved her off. "It's not going to be admitted anyways, so I don't give a damn whether or not there is residue, a blood smear, or a mud stain."

Katz looked at McCarthy. "This is probably the last time I'm going to talk to you," he said. "To say I'm disappointed is an understatement. Your actions are chilling. You made a calculated decision to commit a murder. You planted clues the way that investigators find them and the way prosecutors present them in court. But instead of searching for the truth, you did it to obfuscate the truth.

"You even used me. You tried to stage your confession with Abe Lowenstein, but he threw you out of the house. So you came to me. You confessed to being an accessory when you were actually the murderer. You provided me with bogus emails. And you expected me to be a witness at your forthcoming trial explaining to a jury how you came forward to tell me the truth.

"You are a despicable, sad, desperate person."

Katz departed alone. Stone and Santana remained in the room. This time McCarthy would be taken to jail but he would not be released. McCarthy's eyes glazed over.

Tricia Barton removed the handgun from her dresser. It was a present from her ex-husband. It was the only thing she kept that originally belonged to him. He had told her it might come in handy someday. She went downstairs. She should have left a note, but to whom would she have addressed it? Her only daughter was dead. Her ex-husband was in a nursing home in Florida in lockdown with most of the patients testing positive for the coronavirus. It was probably only a matter of time for him. She pressed the gun to her temple and pulled the trigger.

They would find her boots upstairs in her closet. On the left heel would be blood matching that of her daughter. The same shoe print would be found in the mud outside the sliding glass door. Additionally, there was the digital assistant, hidden in her closet next to the boots. Finally, there were the emails to McCarthy. Let them know the truth. It would not matter any longer to her.

Let them know the whole truth. Let them finally know the poisonous relationship that existed between mother and daughter. Let them feast on how weird we were, looking so much like one another. And let them be sorry for Mac McCarthy, who got himself tangled up with the likes of us. Poor guy.

"Mac," Wolfe said. "Mike McCarthy, can you hear me?" McCarthy appeared to be in a trance. Then he snapped back to attention. "I'll set up a video conference to talk to you in a couple of days." Wolfe said. "I'm not going to go down to the jail. I'm at risk. No offense, but I don't want to die defending you."

Stone looked at the officers and cocked her head. "Take him away," she said.

*

McCARTHY STUCK to his story that he was only an accessory after the fact to Hutton's murder. The woman he claimed to have assisted — Barton — was dead. If it could be shown that McCarthy killed Barton, then the evidence would convict him of a double homicide.

Reese sketched out the case that would have to be put together to convict McCarthy of a double homicide and presented it to Katz, Stone, Santana, and Lin later that day.

To convict McCarthy of both crimes, Reese said, the evidence would have to show that he shot Barton and then staged her suicide. It would come down to the latex glove. The gunpowder residue on the barrel of the gun and on Barton's temple created the appearance that she had taken her own life. But the residue on the latex glove in the department store bag found in McCarthy's home might tell another story.

Barton could have been asphyxiated, Reese theorized. Her fingers could have been wrapped around the trigger. The gun was then placed against her temple. The finger of the unconscious woman was pressed against the trigger and the gun was fired.

If it could be shown that McCarthy shot Barton and made it appear that she had committed suicide, the emails would be damning, Reese explained. On their face, the emails purported to show a series of messages from Barton to McCarthy confirming her role in stabbing her daughter. In the hands of a trained prosecutor, those emails would have convinced a jury that a desperate woman had killed her daughter to win sole possession of her lover.

"Let me show you what is marked as Exhibit A and ask if you recognize it. It is the first indication that Tricia Barton admitted to committing the crime entirely on her own, is that correct? And here is Exhibit B. Is that a further corroboration of her sole design to effectuate the death of her child? And is that amplified by Exhibit C?"

If, however, the evidence convinced a jury that McCarthy shot Barton, then the emails stood for an entirely different proposition, namely that they were composed by McCarthy as part of his orchestrated effort to frame Barton.

Those emails began to appear immediately after Hutton's attack, Reese said. The IT experts would have to show the emails originated from a bogus account owned by McCarthy but created under the name of Tricia Barton and then contoured to appear to originate from her. He used her typeface. He mimicked her tone and style of writing. Since he had received emails from her in the past, it would be easy for him to do. In other words, the emails were really the brainchild of an evil prosecutor who used his courtroom skills to stage a nonexistent crime and to obfuscate his own culpability.

Additional evidence would include the footage from the neighbor's door cam showing a man going to Barton's home with a shopping bag. The bag probably contained the digital assistant and the boots. McCarthy had dipped the heel of the boot in blood and the sole in mud to implicate Barton when he tried to kill Hutton, showing himself to be a despicable and conniving murderer. He then placed the evidence in a closet after he killed Barton.

The digital assistant would be dusted for prints, Reese said. A print might be found on the plug at the end of the cord. McCarthy would have left the print when he pulled the cord from the wall at the time of the stabbing. Although he would have wiped down the device, he might have neglected to wipe the plug.

Yet Reese acknowledged that other incriminating evidence was missing. There was no bloody clothing retrieved from McCarthy's home. True, he probably disposed of it, but there had been blood everywhere and yet no item of his clothing bore any blood. He was captured on camera the following day — ironically, in the video with the U.S. Attorney's office — and there was no evidence of any scratches or bruises on his face.

Despite a plethora of evidence pointing toward McCarthy for the double murder of Jane Hutton and her mother, Tricia Barton, there was a possibility he could end up only being convicted of being an accomplice to Hutton's murder. Katz played the role of defense counsel for the group and explained how it was possible to beat that rap.

Some of the evidence was circumstantial, Katz explained. For example, no one knew what was really inside the shopping bag that was carried to Barton's house. It was pure surmise that the digital assistant and the boots were inside the bag. Furthermore, the person going into her home wore a mask and baggy clothes. Stone had not mentioned that when she brought officers to McCarthy's home to execute the search warrant. It might have been the reason McCarthy looked at her smugly when she mentioned the incident.

If Wolfe could poke holes in the search warrant executed at McCarthy's residence, it was possible that the latex glove could be excluded as evidence and never presented to the jury. If that happened, Katz reminded the others, the ability to show that Barton's death had not been a suicide would be harder to prove.

Finally, some of the evidence would not be considered incriminating at all. For example, if there were fingerprints on the device's plug they could be easily explained once a jury learned that McCarthy spent his weekends at Hutton's place.

Something more was needed. "Motive," Katz said. "Without a motive, a shrewd attorney like Wolfe will create a reasonable doubt in the mind of the jury, or at least in the mind of a single juror." Katz looked at Reese when he said it, remembering their discussion about the Supreme Court decision requiring a unanimous jury verdict. "After all, that's all it takes," Katz said. "One gullible person on the panel could prove to be McCarthy's salvation."

Katz asked Stone to allow his team to search for a motive behind the murders. "We need to look into the facts and circumstances surrounding the civil case concerning Marconi and Simon," he said. "We need to comb through it. If Mac was implicated in that operation, it will explain why he needed to silence Jane. Everything then falls into place."

"Where do we start?" asked Lin.

"Get Jane's phone records," Katz said, "and see if she made any calls on her work phone to either Simon or Marconi. It's possible that Jane reacted to Marconi's message by getting in touch with her."

"I'm on it," Lin said.

*

Six Years Earlier

MIKE McCARTHY came from a blue-collar family. A college degree from U Mass and a law degree from Suffolk were not necessarily the strongest credentials in the world. But it did not matter. McCarthy knew what he was made of, and that it was only a matter of time before he reached the top. He was more aggressive than anyone else. He never complained. And he never stopped trying. If there was a word that typified him, it was persistence. Others might be surprised that he should become the chief of staff to Abe Lowenstein, the chairman of the Senate Intelligence Committee, but it never surprised him.

When Hank Simon's nephew asked for a political favor, McCarthy did not have to be told what to do. He obliged. After all, Hank Simon was a major contributor to Abe Lowenstein's campaigns. And, if the opportunity ever arose, Simon would back Lowenstein to be on a presidential ticket. It might be a few years off — maybe 2024 — but it loomed in the world of the possible.

"I really don't think we should be here," said the contracting officer for HHS. "This smacks of political pressure. It's the sort of thing that gets people into trouble."

They were in the bureaucrat's office. McCarthy had left the Russell Senate Office Building earlier in the day without saying where he was going. Now he was seated in a small, windowless conference room with this weasel. There were three of them gathered for the meeting, which was not recorded on anyone's calendar. The third person was David Simon.

"I don't think there's anything wrong with this arrangement," McCarthy said, "and I don't see why anyone needs to know anything about it. I'm not looking for any favors. I'm looking for a way to help you. Mr. Simon has opened a business in Paterson, New Jersey, to help disadvantaged workers in the inner cities. He needs some seed money to lift his initiatives off the ground. You can provide loans, grants, and contracts. With your help, Mr. Simon can render assistance to thousands of needy people. These people are not seeking a handout — they want a hand up. We're talking about people who never recovered from the last recession. They were left behind when the housing bubble burst and they've never recovered. Now is their chance. Now is your chance to make a contribution and help. Isn't that what you want to do? Isn't that what you were meant to do?"

The bureaucrat knew the score. Simon needed federal money to gain a foothold in the business. Left to his own devices, he'd fail. But if Simon got backing from the financial tools at the government's disposal, he could be guaranteed success.

"I'll see what I can do," he mumbled resignedly.

It was the beginning of a fateful relationship. As Simon received more contracts, McCarthy received invitations to sporting events and weekend junkets, expensive gifts, and an occasional envelope filled with a wad of cash. Once it started, it was impossible to stop. An unsolicited gift became an expected entitlement. To ensure a steady stream of Simon's largesse, McCarthy continued to do favors. He applied pressure on agency personnel to supply Simon with loans under favorable terms. He managed to provide technical drafting assistance to appropriations provisions that benefited Simon. And he introduced Simon to others on Capitol Hill. Soon Simon learned the game. He provided money to political campaigns, particularly to incumbents in safe seats. He hired Marconi as a lobbyist. Given her proximity to powerful interests in D.C., she peddled his interests in the halls of Congress. As a result, more laws were passed with provisions that advantaged Simon.

Thursday, April 11

AFTER GETTING the news from Hutton the previous day, McCarthy put in the call. When Simon answered, McCarthy said, "David, you need to know a whistleblower complaint has been lodged against your company. Someone has complained about your collaboration with Marconi."

Simon was stunned. He knew one of the subcontractors had requested a cut of the action. He assumed Marconi had taken care of it. "How did you learn this?"

"One of our attorneys, Jane Hutton, informed me. I asked her to send the complaint my way. I obtained it from her earlier today. There's no electronic copy. I'll bury it. No one will know anything about it."

"That name is familiar, Mac. Is that the same woman who represented BOM in its case?"

"Yes, that's right. She was named deputy for the civil division shortly after BOM copped to a plea for both criminal and civil charges."

"I can have the chairman of BOM give her a call to cease and desist," Simon said. "You know her, Suzanne Marconi. She's stopped into your office when you used to work for Abe Lowenstein. She does my lobbying on Capitol Hill."

"Not a good idea," McCarthy advised. "Having Marconi call Hutton would only add fuel to the fire. They don't get along. It would only exacerbate the situation."

"Will Hutton follow up and ask what you did with the complaint?"

"Unlikely," McCarthy said. "There's too much going on at the office, particularly now with the coronavirus. On the civil side, she's going to be looking at insurance fraud, business loans, and corporate overreach. She'll be too busy to remember."

"I wouldn't be so sure," Simon said. "She's probably familiar with my cases at Stephens Babcock. It's rumored she downloaded sensitive information about my *modus operandi* onto a thumb drive and took it with her. If that's true, she's got a roadmap to prosecute me."

McCarthy paused. "In other words, you're dead if it's used against you."

"We're both dead," Simon corrected McCarthy.

195

"I'm not sure what you mean."

"Um, it means that you're knee-deep in my shit," Simon laughed. "There's a trail going back six years that includes testimony about your nefarious efforts to help my business. You're not mentioned by name, but the activities are explained in extricating detail."

"Everything I did was legal," McCarthy said.

"If you say so," Simon replied. "Of course, just so you know, that's not what Marconi tells me. She says you crossed the line when you pressured people into awarding me no compete contracts when I started in the business. 'Applying undue influence' or something like that. And the gifts you received from me. Are those supposed to be reported, Mac? And, if they are, did you? Just wondering. Marconi says they're supposed to be in some annual filing. She doesn't think you reported it. I mean, I don't really know much about these things."

"What are you saying?"

"I'm saying that you need to bury that complaint and prevent Jane Hutton from checking anything from past cases against me. I don't care how you do it, just do it."

*

Sunday, April 12

THEY MET on Saturday night at the park and bicycled to her place, as was their normal routine. The weekend was enjoyable. She had picked up fresh produce earlier in the day. Meats had been delivered to her door. They ate dinner by candlelight, streamed an old James Bond movie starring Sean Connery, and made love. Hutton made coffee in the morning. McCarthy was in the shower when she decided to make the call.

"Suzanne, it's Jane Hutton. I'm calling you back about that message you left me Friday."

Marconi was caught off guard. She had not expected a return phone call. She thought her message was clear: back off. There was no need for further discussion. She wondered if Hutton was setting a trap. "Okay," she said. "Are you recording this call?"

"No, of course not," Hutton said. "I just want you to know that your idle threat is not going to dissuade me in the least bit. I'm going to pursue it. Whatever happens, happens."

"You shouldn't act so cavalierly," Marconi replied. "There will be significant collateral damage if anything comes of it. And some of it will blow back on you."

"Collateral damage?" Hutton laughed. "This isn't a military maneuver, Suzanne." She poured herself a cup of coffee and sat at the kitchen island where her computer was set up.

"For one thing, it'll be embarrassing for David's uncle, Hank," Marconi said. "He prides himself in running a tight ship. He studiously avoids controversy. David is the black sheep in the family. You might not care about Hank Simon, but it'll affect his relationship with your mother."

"Suzanne," Hutton said, shaking her head, "none of that matters. You don't shun an investigation into allegations of wrongdoing just because it might affect someone's personal relationship. That's patently ridiculous. Having said that, I'm not surprised to hear it coming from you."

Marconi said, "It'll be viewed as vindictive on your part. People know about your relationship with David. He dumped you, Jane. And people know that you despise me. Plus, it'll bring negative attention to a colleague in your office. Do you want that to happen?"

Hutton took a sip of her coffee. "I'm not following you. Which one of my colleagues? Mo Katz?"

"No, I'm talking about Mike McCarthy."

"What about Mac?"

"You should ask him yourself," Marconi said. "It'll be messy for your office and your boss. And it might engender some ill will towards you as well."

Hutton didn't hear the water stop running in the shower or see McCarthy standing at the bottom of the stairs between the foyer and the kitchen, listening. Hutton continued pressing Marconi for details for several more minutes. Finally, she hung up the phone and tossed it on the counter. "Fuck!" she said out loud.

"What's the matter?" McCarthy asked.

"How long have you been there?" she asked, startled. She narrowed her eyes and stared at him. Then she said, "I know what you did."

"I'm sorry? What I did? What did I do, Jane? What the hell are you even talking about?"

She picked up the coffee cup and gripped it tightly. "Mac, how could you? Well, I'm not sitting on it. I'm going to Mo first thing on Monday and informing him. And, I'm taking it to the IG and to main Justice."

"What are you talking about?"

"You're in cahoots with David Simon, the subject of that whistleblower complaint. I just spoke to Suzanne Marconi. She told me all about you and what you've been doing. Are you the one who told Simon to have her call me?"

McCarthy was stunned. He had taken steps to take possession of the written whistleblower complaint. He was going to wrestle the files away from Lin next week. He had it under control. He told Simon *not* to inform Marconi. *What the hell had happened?*

"We need to talk," he implored her.

"You can talk all you want with Mo. You've got a lot of explaining to do."

"I'm acquainted with Simon but he's never been involved in anything illegal."

"That's a lie, Mac. Like I told you on Wednesday, I've had my eye on Simon for years. He's a client at my old firm. He's a sleazebag. According to what Marconi told me, he was paying you to get state and federal investigators off his back."

"You're way out of line, Jane. You can't believe Marconi."

"Actually, I can. I think Simon has been using your services since the days when you worked for Abe Lowenstein in the Senate."

"This is crazy talk."

"I think you need to leave."

"Oh, give me a break!"

"I don't want anything to do with you. What you've done is scary. I feel as though I never knew you. You're just a weak, pathetic man, that's all you are."

"Please don't talk about me that way."

"I'll talk about you any way I want."

"Listen, Jane, don't be so judgmental. Plus, you're getting yourself into trouble by looking into things connected to your old firm. It's a conflict of interest. I could report you for breaking client confidentiality."

Hutton put down the coffee cup and pulled out a cigarette from a pack that had been lying around for nearly a month. She had stopped smoking when the coronavirus threat emerged, but now she couldn't help herself. "Don't try to play a card like that," she scoffed. "I haven't crossed any line. You're just trying to bluff me. It's an old trick, Mac. It doesn't work on people like me. I'm bulletproof."

"Don't I mean anything to you?"

"Oh, please." She lit the cigarette. "Is that the way it's going to be? You can't bluff me so you're going to try to romance me? I don't believe you! I gave you the complaint on Thursday. Now I know why you wanted it. And I understand why you asked about the whereabouts of the thumb drive and the files from Stephens Babcock. You were going to destroy everything." She hissed her next sentence: "You deceived me."

"I deceived you?" he cried. "You have it backwards. You deceived me. You walked into my life to destroy my relationship with your mother. You acted out of jealousy and spite."

"My mother? What does my mother have to do with this?"

"You always have to one-up her. It's what motivates you to get up in the morning. It's the thing that drives you."

"Oh my God!" she scoffed.

The doorbell rang.

"I'm leaving," McCarthy said, turning to take the stairs to the basement and exit through the sliding glass doors. He was rarely seen in her company. He preferred it that way. And at that moment he saw an advantage to having maintained anonymity.

She put out the cigarette and headed to the door. "I'm beginning to see it all now. Looking back on it, Mac, I think you started our relationship because I came from Stephens Babcock. You knew Simon was a client of the firm. All along, you were watching your own back while you pretended to care about me."

"That's utterly ridiculous," he laughed. "I had no idea that Simon had any connection to your old firm."

"Maybe that's right," she reflected. "But I've noticed something about you, Mac. You're not a prosecutor at all. You're actually a member of the criminal class. You use your training and experience in criminal justice to cover your tracks in your criminal transgressions. You were never a law-and-order type. You came from the Hill. You were only ever about advancing your self-interest."

She looked through the peephole and opened the front door. Judkis was there holding a potted plant. "Hello," she said. McCarthy quickly dipped behind the corner and took the stairs to the basement. "I hope I'm not interrupting anything," Judkis said, seeing the figure behind Hutton. "It's just that it's Easter Sunday and I wanted to drop over and say hello." She peered inside. "Who was that?"

McCarthy ran outside, jumped on his bike, and rode off.

He considered his plight. Hutton sounded like she was definitely going to go to Katz and blow up everything he had worked so hard to keep under wraps. He didn't see any way out of this mess, other than to keep Hutton quiet. And he had to do it quickly. Could he bring her into the scheme with Simon? Have her make nice with Marconi? He considered those possibilities for only a moment before discarding them. He knew her well enough to know she wouldn't go that route. Whatever her faults, she was committed to the rule of law. It seemed there was only one option that would prevent the situation from getting out of control.

He could walk up to her house, knock on her door, enter the house, and kill her. It was as simple as that. "Knock. Talk. Enter. Kill. Exit. Murder." Those were the words written by the man convicted of the Dunning murder.

People never forgot Dunning's case because it was so brazen. It made everyone feel vulnerable. She was killed in broad daylight answering the door to her home. It wasn't until two other similar murders occurred a decade later — Ronald Kirby in 2013 and Ruthanne Lodato in 2014 — that a suspect was apprehended and convicted of her murder.

Ironically, the simplest cases were sometimes the most confounding. If it took a decade and two additional attacks to find Dunning's killer, imagine how hard it might be to solve a similar murder that occurred today? A thorough police investigation could not be conducted speedily because the coronavirus reduced available manpower, depleted forensic resources and lab time, and retarded police investigatory tools, like scrubbing down surfaces. McCarthy could commit a murder and slip away under cover of COVID-19.

He knocked on the door. Hutton answered. He rushed inside. He lowered the knife hidden in his pants pocket and stabbed her in the abdomen. That would be enough to kill her. He provided some window dressing, a series of superficial wounds that would lead investigators to conclude the attacker was probably a woman with less upper body strength. He grabbed the digital assistant from the counter when she called out to it. He removed one of the boots that Tricia Barton had left at his home and dipped it in Hutton's blood as she lay on the kitchen tile floor. He also stuck the boot in the mud outside the patio when he left. He would plant the boots in Barton's home, along with the device and the knife. He grabbed Hutton's phone and turned it off. He would leave that at Barton's as well.

He would write a series of emails from Barton admitting to the crime. It would be enough to incriminate her. If things got messy, he could claim he was an accomplice after the fact. He had a chance of beating the rap and, even if he didn't, he probably would get only a minimal sentence.

McCarthy shook his head, awaking from his dream. They had been occurring with greater regularity over the past weeks. He was scaring himself. He was beginning to question what was real and what was imaginary. Had he actually done those things? Had he just dreamed them? It was as though time was in an hourglass. It kept slipping away. It was becoming harder and harder to put things in perspective.

He started to cry. He trembled. At moments, he felt as though he was in complete control of his actions. At other times, he felt as though he was motivated by forces that he could not control. And at still other times he was uncertain whether the actions he recollected were real or dreams.

*

THE NET was tightening. "Ms. Marconi, my name is Mo Katz, the U.S. Attorney for the Eastern District of Virginia. Do you have a few minutes to talk about Mike McCarthy? I wonder if you can shed some light on his relationship with you and David Simon. This is in connection with a complaint we've received in my office about a subcontractor in Richmond who does some work for you and for Mr. Simon."

Marconi was polite to Katz. She said nothing that would incriminate her. She left the door open for discussion, negotiation, and settlement. She said she needed to talk to her lawyers. Katz said he understood. She thanked him and said she'd be back in touch the next day.

Then Marconi called Simon.

"Stall him," Simon said. "Shred any papers in your possession.

There's been no request for documents, so we can't be accused of meddling with an investigation. Destroy everything!"

"Calm down, David," she said. "Show some of that steely resolve that Uncle Hank is known for. This is not a problem."

"Please don't keep saying that," he begged.

"We're not destroying anything," she said. "The first thing we're going to do is contact Stephens Babcock. Let's get some professional advice. I'd like to see if we can leverage the case in our favor. Katz is looking for information to nail McCarthy. You have it. Plenty of it. If you provide information about Mac's illegal and unethical actions on your behalf, and his receipt of illegal gifts, there's plenty that translates into *motive*.

"That's what Katz is after, don't you see? He's looking for Mac's motivation to kill Hutton. As much as I hated the woman, I never would have sought to hurt her physically. Mac deserves to be put in front of a firing squad. You can give the ammunition. And, in so doing, you can win points."

"What kind of points?"

"The kind of points that prosecutors never talk about when a guilty party assists in an investigation against a guiltier party," she explained.

"You're talking leniency?" he asked.

"Remember our walk along the towpath in Georgetown?" Marconi asked. "You wanted to make the whistleblower complaint go away. Well, we need to confer with Stephens Babcock, but I think I have a plan that might work. All you have to do is tell the truth and nothing but the truth. It'll be incriminating but not injurious, at least not against you. Plus, it'll be payback for what that punk did to Hutton. I detested her, but I hate that guy Mac a hell of a lot more for what he did to her."

*

FUNERALS FOR Jane Hutton and Tricia Barton were

203

postponed because of the coronavirus, but a small graveside ceremony with a few relatives was held at St. Mary's cemetery in Old Town. No one from the U.S. Attorney's office attended except Katz, who showed up just as he had the night he drove to Baltimore nearly two weeks earlier. He felt a shortness of breath as he watched, thinking of the two lives cut short. Mother and daughter both dead within days of each other, following the same pattern to the end. He bowed his head and retreated to his car. Then he drove down to the waterfront near Jones Point.

He parked, got out of the car, and walked around. His shortness of breath was gone. Maybe it was fear that gripped him. Perhaps it was the pollen in the air. He doubted he had the virus. He stood at the water's edge recounting the emotional roller coaster he had ridden the past week. After years of neglecting his parents, he had renewed his relationship with them at a moment when it appeared it might be about to end. By a stroke of fate, his mother survived the coronavirus. At the same time, a trusted colleague had succumbed to it. Perhaps Jane Hutton would have died anyway, but she had not been given a fighting chance. He wondered how all of this happened. How did this disease invade his life and affect the lives of people he loved? Why were some of them spared and others taken?

He composed a silent prayer. It was an expression of gratitude for being alive during a pivotal moment in time. He prayed he would neither fear nor regret the moment and that he would contribute to the greater good. He was not a nurse or a doctor. He could not protect people from getting COVID-19 and he could not cure the people who were dying from it. But he could do one thing. He could make sure people paid for their crimes, even during a time of tremendous upheaval.

As he returned to his car, his phone rang. It was an attorney from Stephens Babcock calling to say that Simon and Marconi would cooperate with investigators and testify if the case against McCarthy went to trial. A minute later, Lin called. She had spoken to Judkis, who admitted seeing McCarthy at Hutton's home the morning of Hutton's murder. Slowly but surely, the case was coming together.

*

"MO, JIMMY WOLFE. I know you're there, my friend. Call me back, will you?" The message on Katz's phone was short and sweet, like Wolfe himself. Katz returned the call a few minutes later. "Why don't you just answer your phone when it rings?" Wolfe asked. "It's your private number. How many crank calls are you gonna get on it?"

Katz knew what Wolfe was up to. "Don't try to schmooze me, Jimmy. I'm not trying the case. You'll be dealing with Stoner and the folks in the Alexandria Commonwealth Attorney's office."

"I know, Mo, but I can't help myself. It's what I do." He laughed, but then turned serious. "Listen, Mo, I just wanted you to know that McCarthy may plead insanity. He's delusional in a big way. I've spoken to him a couple of times and he goes off on these dreamlike trances. It's the weirdest thing I've ever seen. I'm wondering if you ever noticed it at work."

"Are you trying to get me to say something you intend to use in court?" asked Katz.

"No, I didn't call for that reason," Wolfe said. "I wasn't thinking of that. But, since you raise the point, yes, I guess I would use any statement you make as possible testimony if we pursue an insanity defense. Does that affect your willingness to answer me?"

The truth was that Katz had seen a change in McCarthy's level of concentration. He had noticed a distant gaze in McCarthy's eyes and a tendency to fade away as they were talking. At the time, it never occurred to Katz that some sort of psychotic episode was taking place.

"It's a condition known as St. Vitus' Dance, or at least that's what I think it is," Wolfe said. "It might be something else. I'll find an expert who can diagnose it and call it by its appropriate name. For purposes of this discussion, we'll call it St. Vitus' Dance."

"Sounds like a song."

"Well, it actually was, by Black Sabbath. I never heard of it myself, either the song or the disease, until today. Turns out it's some kind of neurological disorder. Andy Warhol suffered a bout of it growing up in Pittsburgh. I'm not saying we're going to use it, but I am letting you know we're likely pleading insanity."

"I'm looking it up now in Wikipedia," Katz said, putting down the phone and doing a search on his laptop. "I found something about a Christian saint named Vitus. It says here he died a martyr. He was one of 14 Holy Helpers of medieval Roman Catholicism. His feast day is June 15 — right around the corner."

"Useful information," Wolfe teased. "Well, hopefully the lockdown will be over by then and we'll all be back to work, doing the St. Vitus Dance. This hiatus is killing my business. My current docket is on hold and people aren't committing crimes out there, so I'm not going to have a lot of new business coming down the pike in the short term."

"Sorry to hear all the bad news," Katz said as he continued to scroll through the article. "It says here that the title 'Saint Vitus' Dance' was given to a neurological disorder called Sydenham's chorea because people danced in front of Vitus' statue when they celebrated his feast day." He closed the screen and picked up the phone. "I don't know whether this is a viable mental health disorder or not, but the way I see it, Mac plotted his actions meticulously. He acted deliberately by using the coronavirus as his accomplice. He calculated that COVID-19 would impede the investigation. He knew it could go unsolved for years. As to the second murder, that was totally calculated on his part. He tried to frame Barton with her daughter's death and to escape punishment by making Barton's death look like a suicide. Good luck in convincing a jury that he was crazy."

As Katz hung up, he knew he would have to be truthful if he was called to the stand in a subsequent trial. Maybe McCarthy was in a psychotic state when he committed the crimes. Perhaps he had been slipping in and out of reality for weeks or even months, undetected by his coworkers. It wasn't for Katz to judge. He would simply have to tell the truth as to McCarthy's behavior.

*

MAC, DEAREST: I don't think I can take much more of it. Day after day. Night after night. It doesn't stop. The guilt. The hurt. I feel so helpless. Why did I allow my emotions to get the better part of me! What have I done? I've destroyed my only child. And I've destroyed the relationship with the only man I ever loved, you. Forgive me! I must end it soon. I don't know how, but I will end it soon. My love paralyzed you into inaction. I now understand that. Thank you for choosing to keep my secret. It has given me time to reflect on my actions. And now I must atone. Goodbye, Mac. Affectionately, Tricia

It was still in her computer, a draft never sent, the killer's confession. Except the email didn't fool anyone. It was only too clear that Mike McCarthy, ace criminologist, had attempted to commit a perfect crime in the age of the coronavirus. No one would have discovered it unless they could collectively piece together the clues that had dropped from the moment following the initial attack on Hutton.

*

"WHEN DID you first begin to suspect Mac?" Lin asked Katz. She was holding the draft email that was found in Barton's computer, the one McCarthy had written after he had killed her and arranged the killing to appear to be a suicide.

"Almost from the moment I first told him about Jane's attack," Katz said. "I reached Mac at exactly 4:15 p.m. I remember the digital clock on the dashboard of my car. He said he'd heard it on the news. But Stone said they were withholding information until they had contacted the family. And I saw a television truck arriving at Hutton's home as I left for Baltimore.

"When I called Mac back, I deliberately asked him how the investigation should be handled. He replied by saying we should look at Jane's family members and any enemies she made at her old firm. He was already setting a trap for her mother, Tricia Barton, who was her only family. He didn't mention significant others, which I thought was strange.

"At the time, I didn't know that he and Jane were romantically involved. Then, when I asked him what he wanted to handle, he selected her caseload at the office. He also suggested that there wasn't going to be much information on that front, which I interpreted as downplaying and diverting attention from something that could be significant.

"When it came time to divide the workload, I disregarded what he said and assigned tasks as I wanted. I asked him to look into Jane's personal contacts. I wanted Santana to delve into her caseload, curious if he was going to uncover something.

"At that point, I had a suspicion, but that was all. I was afraid that I was going to upset the morale of the office if I pointed an accusatory finger at Mac. I also did not want to alert him in the event he was guilty. With the benefit of hindsight, I wish I had acted more quickly. We might have saved Tricia Barton."

Lin shook her head in disgust. "He was watching and monitoring us all the time," she said. "For example, he asked me twice about where I was searching for clues. I never suspected he was only interested in whether I looked at the thumb drive. It really upsets me. He invaded our privacy and played us for fools."

"Mac continually played offense and defense," Katz said. "He always examined the angles and tried to figure out how to exploit them. It's what every good attorney does in preparing for trial. You anticipate every possible move and you develop a response to it. Once the case starts, you're only going to employ a fraction of those moves, but you've got all of them stored in your head. You've anticipated the moment in advance and you're prepared for it."

Katz stopped and looked at his face on the screen. He rubbed the back of his head. He leaned back in his chair. He looked at the images of Lin and Santana, both of whom were looking right at him.

"I think we need a group hug," Lin said. She extended her hands to the screen. Santana and Katz did the same. "In the famous words of Alexandre Dumas," she said, "*Un pour tous, tous pour un. One for all and all for one.* I'm looking forward to the day we're back together. I guess this will have to suffice until then."

"We can turn over the case to Stone and the Alexandria Police now," Katz said. "The city will prosecute Mac under state law. I'm not sure whether they'll go for capital murder. They will certainly go for murder in the first degree. Jimmy Wolfe is going to be tough. This case is far from a lock."

*

THE RAIN returned Thursday night. The air was cool. Katz stood under the overhang of the townhouse on a brick step leading to the patio. He was barefoot. The brick was cold against the balls of his feet. Raindrops splashed against his toes. Abby was upstairs. Rain fell in big, fat drops that struck the roof and the patio furniture.

He stepped into the rain, which quickly dampened his clothes. His hair and scalp were soon soaking wet. He closed his eyes and lifted his head. The water washed over his eyelids, cheeks, and mouth.

In the past two weeks, three people who mattered to him had wrestled with issues of life and death. One was his mother. She survived. The second was the deputy of his civil division, Jane Hutton. She had fought to stay alive, first by willing herself to her front door after suffering a severe stab wound and then by struggling to survive after undergoing surgery. Despite her valiant effort, she was dead. The third was the deputy of his criminal division, Mike McCarthy.

209

While McCarthy had not been struck down, he was dead to Katz.

You cannot control every aspect of your life, Katz thought to himself. During a pandemic, you can take steps to avoid catching the virus. You can maintain social distance and wear a mask in public. But you can't trick fate. If you have a pre-existing medical condition or simply find yourself in the wrong place at the wrong time, you can succumb to the coronavirus.

By the same token, you cannot always avoid the irrational impulses and illogical actions of others, Katz thought. Hutton opened her door to McCarthy without any premonition that he was going to lunge at her with a knife. There she was, taking precautions against any unforeseen virus while simultaneously exposing herself to a friend and lover.

Everyone is vulnerable all the time. Life can be taken in an instant by an unseen virus or by a deranged person. No amount of preparation can safeguard everyone from the known villain lurking around the corner and the unforeseen one lingering in the air.

An asymptomatic person can carry a virus and unknowingly pass it to others. A person who appears normal can just as easily sneak up and pull a gun or a knife and destroy one's life. Sometimes the motivation is a festering anger, while other times it is an undiagnosed mental illness. Still other times it's a virus catching a ride on someone's back before jumping off on you. There is a killer behind someone's eyes and in the breeze rippling along the sidewalk. It's always there waiting.

Vulnerability made life previous, Katz thought. The fact that it could be unexpectedly taken at a moment's notice was a reason to celebrate it. Nothing should be taken for granted, he told himself, and everything should be done to safeguard others. He had reestablished contact with his parents. Now that his mother was convalescing, he needed to check on her and try to get up to the Hudson Valley before the end of the year.

Maybe that's what it was all about. Just as a mask was worn to avoid passing the coronavirus to others rather than to safeguard the person wearing it, perhaps the key to protecting oneself in society was to be vigilant toward others. Katz had helped hundreds of criminal defendants like Blair Craig and they had reciprocated by helping others in kind. He hadn't thought of himself when he had helped them but now he realized that he was a beneficiary of his own good deeds. Maybe repairing broken relationships and caring about others was the best way to stay safe.

Katz stood still for a long time, the rain saturating his clothes and hair and covering his body. Then he turned and reentered the townhouse. The number of U.S. deaths from COVID-19 was ticking up to 50,000. By the morning, he knew it would pass that milestone. He wondered how many other milestones would be passed before it ended.

Epilogue

MIKE McCARTHY's TRIAL for the murders of Jane Hutton and Tricia Barton resulted in a hung jury.

The outcome caught everyone by surprise. Wolfe was declared a genius by the media and members of the defense bar. Courthouse observers shook their heads as to how the Commonwealth Attorney's Office could have flubbed the case. Some speculated it was only a matter of time before McCarthy asked to be reinstated in his job as head of the criminal division.

McCarthy pleaded not guilty to both murders. To the extent he was alleged to be an accessory after the fact to Hutton's murder, he pleaded temporary insanity.

In pre-trial motions, Wolfe succeeded in suppressing the evidence found at McCarthy's home, including the latex gloves and the bag with smears of blood and mud.

At trial, Wolfe offered an expert witness who concluded Barton committed suicide. The prosecution's expert inferred strongly that the suicide was staged but could not rule out the possibility that Barton had killed herself.

Since the contents of the bag were inadmissible, the prosecution did not introduce the boots, digital assistant, and phone in its case. But Wolfe did, along with the set of cutlery located in Barton's kitchen with a knife missing in the butcher block. By offering those exhibits in the defense case, Wolfe created the illusion that the prosecution had withheld evidence to mislead the jury.

Wolfe also got an expert to testify that the blades on the knives in Barton's cutlery set were consistent with the cuts sustained by Hutton during the attack.

The prosecution did introduce the emails that McCarthy had shown Katz, along with the email in his 'In' box and the draft email in Barton's computer. A forensic expert testified for the prosecution that all of the emails originated from McCarthy's email account.

However, the defense countered with its own IT expert who said it was conceivable Barton could have made it appear as though the emails originated from McCarthy's account even though she had created them.

McCarthy testified. He admitted that he learned about Barton's attack against her daughter after the fact and failed to take any action to notify law enforcement authorities.

While McCarthy acknowledged his purported role in aiding Barton after she murdered her daughter, he pled temporary insanity. There were dueling mental health experts. Neither side mentioned St. Vitus' Dance, which Wolfe never brought up after mentioning it to Katz.

Under Virginia law, it was left to the jury to decide whether McCarthy was of sound mind.

Despite the complexity of the trial — McCarthy pled temporary insanity for assisting Barton in Hutton's murder while the Commonwealth claimed he committed both murders — eleven jurors voted to convict McCarthy on two counts of murder in the first degree.

However, one juror held out. He was persuaded that Barton committed suicide after murdering her daughter and that McCarthy was out of his mind when he acted as an accomplice after the fact. As a result, a unanimous verdict could not be entered in either case.

The sole juror refused to find McCarthy guilty despite a plethora of evidence that showed McCarthy subverted the investigation, suppressed the whistleblower complaint, and doctored the tape recording played to Katz after McCarthy sent Lin on an errand during one of their video conferences. The evidence also showed that McCarthy did not tell the others about Judkis and pretended to be have technical difficulty with his phone when, in fact, he deliberately ended a video call so that Judkis would not recognize him.

David Simon and Suzanne Marconi both testified against McCarthy. Wolfe made mincemeat of them. Simon was not credible once Wolfe showed he may have been engaged in fraud in the midst of the coronavirus. Marconi was viewed as vindictive. Wolfe played the tape of her calling Hutton, which was enough to lead some jurors to wonder whether she had something to do with Hutton's demise.

No promise was made in advance of trial to Simon and Marconi, but there was an implicit understanding that they would not be prosecuted federally if they testified at the state trial against McCarthy. No charges were ever filed against either of them and the whistleblower complaint was dismissed.

Katz's team was devastated and deflated by the outcome of the case. They overcame roadblocks posed by COVID-19 only to see the case fall apart due to Wolfe's superior lawyering and a single holdout on the jury panel.

Katz was disappointed with the hung jury. If he had been called to testify, he would have acknowledged that McCarthy acted oddly in the weeks prior to the murder by fading in and out of conversations, as though in a daze. But he did not feel McCarthy was clinically insane and he was convinced that McCarthy had committed both murders.

Wolfe called Katz after the trial ended. He reminded Katz that they once taught a legal education seminar together. "I don't know whether you remember it," Wolfe said, "but you told the group that the single most important part of a trial is *voir dire*. I didn't agree with your view at the time, but with the benefit of hindsight, I think you were right."

Katz had no rebuttal to that comment.

Katz missed Hutton, as did everyone in the office. Sally Orr was named acting head of the civil division. Orr restored a semblance of normality in an abnormal time but the void remained from Hutton's absence. The deputy's position for the criminal division remained vacant. Ryan Long applied for the position but was summarily removed from the pool of candidates.

Because McCarthy was not acquitted, the prosecution vowed

to retry the cases. At that juncture, Wolfe folded. If the cases were retried, Wolfe knew the prosecution would successfully counter every trap he had laid the first time around. Furthermore, it was unlikely there would be another outlier on the jury panel.

The plea agreement was tempered. Both sides were skittish about their chances. As a result, McCarthy agreed to a sentence of 20 years to each of two murder counts, with the sentences run concurrently.

Life continued.

Blair Craig emerged from his apartment and went on a date with his online friend. A month later, they moved in together. She had been living with her parents in Leesburg after abandoning New York City. Everyone was delighted.

Snowe found a bidet online and had a plumber install it.

The coronavirus continued to wreak havoc. Katz's neighbors posted a sign in their window that read, "We are all Howard Hughes now!" It was a reference to the reclusive billionaire rumored to have once spent months in a darkened room surrounded by Kleenex boxes. Katz imagined other neighbors with similar signs reading "We are all J.D. Salinger" or "We are all WACO." He hoped it wasn't going to turn out that way.

The truth was that no one knew what lay ahead. The only thing for certain was that there was no returning to the old normal.

Acknowledgements

"Write it Down. Keep a Pandemic Journal." That was the headline of an op-ed piece that appeared in *The Washington Post* on April 25, 2020, by Ari L. Goldman, a journalism professor at Columbia University and author of *The Late Starters Orchestra*. I took his advice to heart, except I didn't write a journal. I wrote the third volume of the Mo Katz mystery series.

Slaters Lane allowed me to memorialize a moment in time unlike any other and preserve it for posterity in the guise of a detective story. I was isolated from others, totally reliant upon technology. Communications with the outside world were conducted primarily through video conferencing programs. I wore sweatpants and T-shirts almost all the time, showered and ate at odd hours, and stepped off sidewalks whenever I was outside and saw someone headed in my direction.

Having written two Mo Katz mysteries, I tried to imagine how his investigation would be impacted by the coronavirus. I also tried to provide historic context with facts and figures of real events occurring in April 2020. Everyone had their unique way of surviving during the pandemic. For me, it was hunkering down with Mo Katz and company.

When the coronavirus hit, I was in the middle of a tour promoting my second book, *Jones Point*. It abruptly stopped in mid-March. I miss bookstores and hope to meet new friends and book lovers as stores reopen and we embrace our new "normal."

Special thanks to people who helped me launch and promote the Mo Katz mystery series in the months preceding the onslaught of the coronavirus. They include Dayna Wilkinson, D.C. Chapter Head, Harvardwood, an organization of Harvard graduates involved in the arts; Beth Lawton, publisher, and Mary Ann Barton, editor, of *Alexandria Living Magazine*; and Mary Wadland, publisher, and Ralph Peluso, literary critic, of *The Zebra Press* in Alexandria, VA.

Also, thanks to the wonderful folks at The Principle Gallery on King Street in Old Town who hosted the release party for *Jones Point*, including Michele Marceau, Clint Mansell, Owen French, and Leigh Palmer.

As always, my gratitude to my publisher Clarinda Harriss and my editor Charles Rammelkamp. Alex White proofread the manuscript and made valuable comments and edits throughout the story. Mark Jung handles distribution of my books with Itasca Books/BookHouse Fulfillment and makes sure they end up where they're supposed to be in advance of my appearances. The man does magic! Bookmobile prints Mo Katz mysteries and I thank Arna Wilkinson, Devin Koch, and the entire crew at the Minneapolis facility.

My love to our sons Alex, Andrew, and Aron, who inspire me every day through their creativity, productivity, and ingenuity. And my devotion to Robin T. Herron, my wife and my best friend, who was my literary editor when we attended Marquette University together and who edits my Mo Katz mysteries today. Thank you, sweetheart!

Thank you for reading this book. If you have any comments, email me at AlendronLLC@aol.com. Tell me what you liked about the story and how I can improve the characters and plots in future stories. I would love to hear from you.

Stay well. Stay safe. And love and peace to those you hold dear.

Mo Katz will return in *Roaches Run*.

Nicole Lacroix Narrates *Slaters Lane*

Nicole Lacroix narrates the audiobook edition of *Slaters Lane*, available online from audiobook distributors and your favorite bookstore. Nicole is the afternoon on-air host of Classical WETA 90.9 FM in Washington, D.C., where she lives with her husband and Labradoodle.

Nicole Lacroix/Credit: Risdon Photography